Liberty's

EXCESS

Liberty's
EXCESS

FICTIONS
LIDIA YUKNAVITCH

FC2
Normal/Tallahassee

Published by FC2 with support provided by Florida State
University, the Unit for Contemporary Literature of the
Department of English at Illinois State University, the Program
for Writers of the Department of English at the University of
Illinois at Chicago, and the Illinois Arts Council

Address all inquiries to: Fiction Collective Two, Florida State
University, c/o English Department, Tallahassee, FL 32306-1580

ISBN: Paper, 1-57366-084-1

Library of Congress Cataloging-in-Publication Data
Yuknavitch, Lidia.
   Liberty's excess:short fiction/by Lidia Yuknavitch.--1st ed.
   p.cm.
   ISBN 1-57366-084-1 (pbk.)
   I. Title.

 PS3575.U35 L5 2000
813'.54--dc21

                                   00-027715

Cover Design: Polly Kanevsky
Book Design: Michelle Citro and Tara Reeser

Produced and printed in the United States of America
Printed on recycled paper with soy ink

Illinois ARTS Council
AN AGENCY OF
THE STATE OF ILLINOIS

This program is
partially sponsored
by a grant from the
Illinois Arts Council

FOR KATHY ACKER. HERE'S TO DEAD THINGS GIVING US LIFE.

"NOTHING'S EVER WRONG. AND I'M NEVER SMASHED."

ACKNOWLEDGMENTS

"Bravo America" appeared in *Ms.*

A section from "Waiting to See" appeared online at *The Iowa Review.*

A section of "Shadow Boxing" appeared in *Other Voices.*

"Cusp" appeared in *Zyzzyva.*

"Blood Opus" appeared in *Fiction International: Terrorisms.*

"Beauty" appeared in *ART:MAG.*

Citations within "Citations of a Heretic" borrowed in pastiche form from literary history. And from *Saint Joan of Arc* by V. Sackville-West.

CONTENTS

ALLEGIANCE

Bravo America

First thing in the morning, when I take out the trash, I see it: syringe on the lawn. Still bloody. Surreal, isn't it. First memory like a shot in the vein. Four long years of youth sliding cold silver glint into waiting blue.

My neighborhood is turning. You know what I mean. It's no big deal, it's no more or less real than TV, than the places I have lived, than all those little white-lined streets running for all they're worth like tracks trying to run off an arm. We can feign a nation of shock all we want, it's still an old story. Somebody wants something more than their own life. Somebody else is terrified by all that want.

I teach literature in college now. My neighbors all have enough money. We don't say the word "bourgeoisie" in America, so I'll just say middle class. But we all know there is no such thing as middle class. There is a preoccupation with respectability and material values all right, and there is a mediocrity of us all running around wearing our consumerism like little brand name helmets, but cmon' now, let's be frank. We want protection like soft warm cocoons. For example, what do they do in my neighborhood? What else, the dreaded *neighborhood watch*. Guy down the street stops me one night as I'm heading home lead-armed with groceries—keep in mind he's never spoken to me in his life; in fact, I've never seen him poke his mole head out of his white house—anyway, he stops me, and he's bobbing his head around like a scared rodent and his eyes are darting out of their sockets and he says it. He's so titillated he is sweating. Have you noticed the *problem?* What problem. You know. He looks one way then the other. I'm thinking, go ahead, no cars are coming, we are on our own street, we are in front of our own houses. He continues. All the dope peddling. The drug deals. And that woman being paraded up and down the street all day all night every day every night. There is a long pause while we consider this.

Who could miss it? What moron wouldn't notice? Not because they're doing anything TO us, but because they're doing it too NEAR us. And isn't that just America all over? This is my house. My street. My neighborhood.

An image: the needle against the flesh threatens with its obscenity—its sterility, its mechanism of invading living skin.

I carry my groceries back to my house. Clark, my other neighbor, the one across the street who lives with his mother and wears undersized rock concert T-shirts and the exact same baseball cap every day of his life, a guy who inherited his money from an accident at work which works and works him over into bitter and pale and beer-bellied and pot-eyed, waves to me from across the street. He crosses and stands on my lawn. He says to me, talking about the drug deals just across the tracks, they'll never change, it's like I always say, once a junkie, always a junkie. I feel anger welling up in my belly and for an instant I want to hurl all my knowledge at him like obscenities. Instead of saying shut the hell up you fucking ignorant asshole I want to say Keats, Byron, Shelly, Van Gogh, Bacon, Eliot, Faulkner—I feel this whole list of famous "M's" rise up my throat for god knows what reason—Mozart Mingus Monk Munch Miller Milo and Malcolm even—I want to move on to Germans, French, Swiss, periods, genres, I want to say if we didn't have junkies we wouldn't have art, but I don't, I just stare at him until he turns away and walks silently back to his yard, his porch, his door, inside. What the hell am I going on about? It's just *Clark*. Why am I so worked up? I turn back toward my own house. Then it hits me: we are alike in our silences and I am stunned.

I manage to make it inside. My husband is in there. He is in his room-made-into-a-studio, painting. We don't make enough to rent him studio space. So we do what we all do. We invent ways to live what we cannot have. I set the groceries down with great relief. Not because I am tired, but because I know he is responsible for dinner, because never again in my life do I have to be responsible for dinner. This is part of my love for him. Sounds dumb, I know, but you'll never know the relief a junkie or a woman can feel when the pressure of the giant script-life begins to lift. God how I love him.

And he loves me too, because I can kiss the scar on his wrist like it bleeds a sweet white sugar. You see, we are learning to live in these houses, these lives. We are loving over our outcast and beaten hearts. For the longest time, neither of us could afford therapy, insurance, or any other route to wellness. Today we probably could afford a health fix for at least one of us, but neither of us has that much investment in the sicknesses. Just as well.

Cherise, the woman on the other side of us, waddles out to feed her cats. A great lumbering woman who is all heart. As if the body puffed her out from all that heart. Our dog ate one of her cats. Well, he didn't really *eat* the thing, just killed it. We don't know exactly how many cats she has over there. We suspect our dog will eat some more in time. Cherise understands. She goes inside. She will come out at exactly 6:30 a.m. and start the Suburu and go to work. She will come home at exactly 5:20 p.m. and go inside. Every day. On Friday one half hour before the garbage truck comes she will put her trash in the can. One time, out of the blue, she asks us if we want some poppies. She says she has some bulbs from somewhere in Asia and then she lowers her voice. You know, she hushes, the *funny* kind.

I'm sitting on the couch and there she goes by. The woman being paraded up and down the street. He is skinny with desperation and she is skinny with fatigue. Both have the ashen flesh of heroin. I feel like I know them in the dumbest way. They are always swearing. She is always following him. Up the street. Down the street. And then again. Sometimes I just think of one word: cadaverous. I used to think, the closer you get to death, that's where the life is. Now I watch from inside my house through a plate glass window. I hear my husband pissing in the toilet. The ordinary sound is enough to bring me to my knees. I want to say, thank you, thank you, thank you.

I see a guy come out of the alley right after them, buttoning his goddamn fly. I think, the thing about the 1990s is that we have no irony, no subtlety, no reason to allegorize anything. Jesus, buttoning his fucking fly and heading on down the road. How is it that America can say anything with a straight face? I watch the man and the woman walk like sticks out of sight.

An image: withdrawing the needle, the skin slides itself closed leaving just this tiny red hole.

Later, I'm inside, the living room window just plain glass against the night. Phyllis, across the street, is at it again. She waters her flowers and yard at about 11:30 p.m. every night. She's bent and rounded in the back from age, but she still looks feisty. She's got her white hair in a sassy little bun on top of her head. Once I saw her march over to the couple yelling at each other on the corner and tell the guy he was just an arrogant loud mouth. He took a step toward her and she didn't budge. Five-foot-nothing and she just stood there, kind of bent-over and with the eyes of a roach: You ain't never gonna get rid of me buster, I can outlive the ice age, I'm gonna live to be one hundred and ninety years old.

Next time I see them I am alone in the house. I am in the living room on the couch. I am reading student journals. I encourage them to write about what scares them.

14

Turns out nothing much scares them. AIDS, not getting a job, babies. I am in this one journal that is different. I am on this one sentence: and I feel like I'm invisible and then I hear all kinds of noises. I cannot remember the face of the student. I look up. There they are. Just like punctuation. I can hear the refrain of the sentence. Sometimes I feel like I'm invisible and then I hear all kinds of noises. Why why why always why from mother, from father, from therapist, from doctor, from counselor, from teachers, from friends, from lovers, why why why. This time I see her face: cadaverous. I fly out the door. They stop. I know exactly what they are seized by as I wave to them: what the hell does she want? She is not a man.

How much.

15

What?

How much for her. How much for an hour.

Let's get the fuck outta here, she says.

Look. I've got one hundred dollars. I want an hour. One hundred bucks is one hundred bucks, isn't it?

He looks down the street. He looks at her. She's got gimme a fucking break on her face. She doesn't look at me once. He looks back down the street, thinks he sees someone, then doesn't. Finally he shoves his open hand toward me to her Jeeeeezus fucking Christ.

But a deal's a deal, and he shuffles off a bit after giving her some kind of stare down. I'm back home for a long second, but she doesn't know it. Like a transplanted heart I live on this street in this life with this job and these neighbors always in danger of the body rejecting me. Come inside my house.

There are no names. Some people understand this. She stands there with her bony arms in a knot across her chest. She has long stringy hair permed a year ago. Dark circles cupping worn-out gray eyes. Some sweater from 1972. Bell-bottom jeans. Jean-jacket tied around her waist, pulling your eyes down to the floor. You don't want to look her in the eye and you can't help looking her in the eye.

Sit down.

I don't want to—what the fuck do you want with me?

YUKNAVITCH

Lidia

Sit down.

She sits down.

This is what me a woman who teaches English thinks looking down at a woman who sucks dicks all day and all night every night as she sits on my couch. This is what me an x addict reformed by love and understanding and given something to believe in because of books thinks looking at her. This is what me who could not stand to be alone in a room with just me thinks: she looks like Mary. This is what Mary must have looked like after Jesus. No way for the body to bear the miracle, the burden, the unbelievable history of nothing. When I see an image of Christ I picture a Mary so drawn and gaunt and tired and angry to the point of emaciation that she can barely wear her own face.

She smokes. Her shaking is familiar between us. What do I think I am going to do, teach her?

I've got this woman in the house. I have one hour. Sometimes all the hours of life we have lived rip—only an instant—then suture back up as if nothing ever entered.

Something in common: you can't stare a whore or a junkie down. Either they look away, making you think you are invisible, making you think you fell off the goddamn globe altogether, or they stare through your skull and out the other side leaving a gaping hole where your psyche used to be, and you are left some hollowed out moron afraid of crazy people, afraid of ghosts, afraid of your own, relentless shadow. We stare each other down until she says look man, what's this all about? You want something? Smoke? Smack? Horse? You want me to do something? This is fucking weird. She takes another drag and quivers like an angel. No, not like an angel. Like an ordinary woman being eaten alive by her own heart, her own veins, her own cunt.

I say look, and I step toward her and put my hand near her neck and shoulder as gently as I can and she says I don't fucking lick pussy. I'm not into that shit. But I'll play with your tits if you want. I feel more stupid and cacophonously deaf than I've ever felt in my life. I look at

16

her for a long minute. I drop my hand to its ignorance. What does one say back to words like that? Finally I tell her that I just wanted to give her an hour break. Rest. Eat. Sleep. Drink. Smoke. Do whatever you want. She looks at me like I am out of my fucking mind, her mind bolts toward the door. I guess you can leave too, if that's really what you want. That's really what she wants, but she stays.

Nothing happens for exactly one hour. Nothing. And aren't you just a little disappointed? Weren't we all hoping for something else? What a lousy movie our lives would make.

I leave the room, so I don't know if she slept or ate or what. Here is what I do: go to my computer and write like crazy. I know I can write without stopping like I know addiction. I don't think I feel benevolent but I'm afraid I might. I think of the most stupid things in the universe I want to do for her and I write them down. Play her Schubert, wash her hair, give her a foot rub, cook her a real French dinner with six courses, give her my vintage crepe silk dress, watch Catherine Deneuve movies with her, read stories by Colette to her, paint her fingernails, dunk her in a luxurious bubble bath, give her all the money in my savings account, buy her a plane ticket, take photos of her and last but not least, hold her. I come back an hour later positively fevered and swelling with compassion and she's standing there plain and unimpressed. S'that it is all she wants to know. Yeah, I say, that's it. And then she's gone, he's there to meet her down the street, there is another guy there too, they walk off and become smaller and smaller in sight as if they are walking back to childhood.

My husband returns. Do I tell him? Once a junkie, always a junkie. I tell him. He is mildly furious. Well, actually, he's kind of turned on. I mean, on the other side of his worry that they will come back and rape and kill me and burn down the house is this kind of erotic curiosity, you know, a whore in the house and we're thirtysomething white teachers, pretty little white artists in their bordering-on-dangerous neighborhood with their inconsequential middle class neighbors looking through plate glass

17

free writing scene

windows like fat owls. During dinner he keeps sneaking peeks out the window into the black nothing. I guess we might both be hoping she'll come back to us. That something will happen. I guess that has its own sweetness. An American sweetness: find something to save. Find something to kill.

The last dangerous thing we did was load up on mushrooms and wander out into the streets of our own neighborhood. At the tracks a train brushed by like wind and I just grabbed on and jumped up. He stood there. He told me that he watched me cling to the train like an insect until I disappeared into motion and night. Eventually I came to and let go and did a kind of strange and complex military roll into a pile of gravel. The bruises and cuts left on my body told such a funny story. I journeyed maybe 100 yards. He stood still as night thinking: my wife is a train.

Did she tell him? The guy she came with, the guy she left with? I keep wondering. Nothing to tell, really. Maybe it creeped her out, maybe a guy's hands and slobber and dick are ordinary and familiar and a woman who gives you an hour of nothing is a wacko. Could be; I remember a different logic in my body, even if my mind is beginning to forget. It's the body that pulls you to the next hour, not the mind. It's the mind that makes up stories to cover for the body, so the body won't be found out as the junkie it is.

I am drinking a scotch. No big deal, just drinking a scotch. My husband is in his pretend studio, painting. She has been gone a week. I am watching TV, trying to recognize something.

And then I see them, through my living room plate glass window like a giant screen I see them passing in the night. The neighborhood watch. I hear the murmur of low voices just out of my vision, or is it the TV in the background? I turn from the images on the set to the image of the walkers still fuzzing over vision. Their flashlights swing back and forth with purpose and conviction. They've all purchased some kind of Day-Glo vests and matching orange caps.

Women with children are packed into the middle of the group, men on the outsides. Their heads bob with the passion of their mission. They do not look afraid. They are all wearing different forms of Nikes that glow like lowly beacons with every step. They are perfect in their movements, synchronized, beautiful. They will cover maybe five blocks north and south and five east and west. Manifest destiny. There is no one suspicious on the corner tonight. There is no one dangerous in the alley. Our streets are quiet and empty, people venture out onto their porches, children ride trikes on the sidewalks. It is one hour of safe and sound. We are warmed like a summer out of time. Our streets are clean and cured and uncultured—no, that's not what I meant at all, uncluttered, I meant uncluttered.

19

Ironie

Honest / Simple / realistic

Waiting to See

culture

Phrase you see everyday

1. The Alchemy of the Melting Pot

In my car. My red Toyota Corolla. Exhaust hums in front of me, behind me. Little voices scratch out of giant boxes with writing on them. Money is readied in the hands of drivers. The sun dips down into her wallow; evening descends on a line of cars in the drive-thru at McDonald's.

A tiny little man in the distance. I can see him in my rearview, just above the words "objects in mirror are closer than they appear." He is on the move, window to window, car to car. In the rearview I can see the faces of other drivers pinch-up as he nears their cars. They dread him. Already they are cringing, scrunching up their shoulders, locking their doors, working buttonholes with their asses in the vinyl seats, trying desperately to look at something else. Anything but the approaching man, bearded, hair in an argument with itself, slightly dirty, rumpled and clearly week-worn clothes, white. He is a white male, maybe thirty-five, maybe forty-five.

By the time you get to the black young man in the first window, huge waves of relief send a shiver up your back. You've made it to the first window, goddammit, and there is an angel there to take your money. There is no room, in other words, for the nasty white man begging money to come around to your driver side window, he simply can't fit between the ledge of the window with the angel taking your money and the safety of your car, its window down, your finger on the button to electronically raise it should danger appear. The young black man takes your money and returns your change, asks you what kind of sauce you want, gives it to you in a little and beautiful white bag with golden arches on it, why, it's heaven, it's just like being in heaven, the delight is filling your whole body now, earlier you thought you had to pee and the line of cars seemed unbearable, but now, now you are making an exchange that is simple and good and profound in its truth. The young black man smiles and waves as you head slowly to the second window, his cap is clean, his teeth are big and white, his salary doesn't even enter your mind, you are free, you are on the way to the second window.

Surely he is at one of the cars behind you. Surely things will get held up there, someone will refuse to open their window and he will knock on it, or he will appear inside the frame of the front windshield and the driver will divert their gaze, he will give up and move on, or back, or away. You risk a quick look in your rearview—nothing nothing nothing like pennies from heaven.

Your car almost magically glides along to the second window, its opening apparent, hands visible, a bag of food bulging and white and smelling of good oil—all vegetable oil—and fried things. Your family is waiting. Your car is filled with gas. The money has been paid.

A pimply-faced girl with headgear and braces hands you your bag, but you see capitalism and youth emerging from the window, you see her first summer job, her first lessons at responsibility and a savings account and taking care of herself, you see her on her way to college, yes, that's it, the summer before college, the lessons she is learning, what a good student she will make, how she will excel in school, how she will learn well, how she will enter the workforce with a good head on her shoulders. And then there is a rapping at your window on the passenger side, and strange how you forgot, isn't it? And your head swivels over out of dumb instinct, and there he is, his bad teeth and leathery skin and marble-blurred eyes filling the window, like a close-up, magnified, terrifying. His horrible mouth is opening and closing, he is saying something to you, he is talking to you, his muffled voice breaking through the glass shelter, now he is yelling, you are clutching your bag for dear life, you are putting your car in drive, his fingers at the ledge of your world, your own body like a snake's: all spine and nerve.

22

Then a new image; from the front window you see a man in uniform, my God, a Korean man with a McDonald's uniform complete with cap and manager's badge is running toward your car, he is waving his arms, he is shouting. With one hand you are clutching your steering wheel as in a near-miss accident and with the other hand you are clutching your white McDonald's bag heavy and full and your eyes are like a deer in the headlights and your body is taut and your nipples are hard as little stones. Your mouth is dry and you are as alert as you are capable of being. The Korean manager yells at the shitty little begging white man, you go now. You go now. You outta here, now. Shithead. Motherfucking. You go. No slaving here. The slip doesn't even phase you. You are with him. United. You are grateful. There is no dividing you. The two of you are in it together, you are saving one another, you are making the world a better place, you are the American way embodied, you are at each other's backs, you are one hundred million served.

2. An Arresting Moment

I was working with a student of physiognomy, biology was her primary major, I believe, but physiognomy was a more accurate nomenclature for the kinds of ideas and work she involved herself with. Suffice it to say, *of the body*, in the scientific sense, particularly in the sense of science as an art, as it were, the way it used to be, historically speaking. As in the art of argumentation or the art of philosophy, the art of science was a practice. Do you see? I worked with her on the weekends, I tutored her in a way, though I do not think that this is an accurate description of the kind of travail we busied ourselves with. One must endeavor to be precise. Let me think now. I believe what we did can best be articulated by means of physics, now bear with me, this all comes to an important end. The two of us together in our weekends of labor formed a kind of intellectual chiasmus. That's it. That is the precise word for it. What I brought from my island of knowledge included a hermeneutics generally foreign to her, a landscape of literature and critical theory which she understood at the level of discourse, and what she brought to her divine study was a system organized around the pursuit of quantifications and objective analyses. Why, the description alone dizzies. Does it not? The eyes lolling back in their little sockets.

At any rate.

She'd been working through an idea with microscopes and controlled experiments that had locked her in her tracks; that is, she had been so stunned by something she'd found, so paralyzed by a moment of what can only be described as the uncanny, in the Freudian sense, of course (if you will permit me a brief aside, the point should not be lost, partly because of the weight of the idea and partly because I owe her the courtesy of giving a full and true account to the listener; an example from the Greek, yes? The story is, that Leontius, the son of Aglaion, coming up one day from the Piraeus, under the north wall on the outside, observed some dead bodies lying on the ground at the place of execution. He felt a desire to see them, and also a dread and abhorrence of them; for a time he struggled and covered his eyes, but at length the desire got the better of him; and forcing them open, he ran up to the dead bodies, saying, "look, ye wretches, take your fill of this fair sight.") and I say Freudian in terms of the uncanny, but one might just as easily refer to Spenserian motifs, looking, the desire to look, the nature of allegory, or Kant, in terms of the nature of the sublime. But I digress. What I mean to allude to here, or to provide the backdrop for, is a sense of the distance between seeing and saying, for that is what she came upon, and that is what the nature of our shared encounter animated.

You see, it happened one day in our work, and here it must be said that she was convinced at the moment of her insight, or perhaps more accurately, her blindness, that she had to move from one architecture of knowledge to another, else be silenced forever, her idea lost to the stars and to more imaginative constellations than physics provided her. Put simply, she saw that she needed to write a book surrounding the *metaphoric* possibilities which surrounded her findings, in addition to continuing her scientific pursuits. This is a striking point. She saw that she needed to work within as well as extend a metaphoric cosmology. For her the reasons were twofold: in the first place she became convinced that her scientific study had no mobility, no course of meaningful action until she cleared the way through creative, if foreign means, and in the second instance she understood with a rare clarity that the metaphoric was a language without which her studies would be bankrupt, bankrupt in the sense of being limited to surfaces and void of intuitive realms. I can assure you that she did not learn this from the institutions inside of which she toiled. It was pure instinct. Something in her denied the path and the system which guided her, and though she could not abandon them, she knew the divergence was a matter of life and death. Intellectually speaking, of course (though one could indeed argue that for those of us who are given life only through synaptic firings, death has a variety of forms, do you see?).

Here the crux: she'd identified a muscle in the body which could neither be seen nor quantitatively analyzed. *Cette muscle*, however and ironically, was responsible for several motor controlled exercises as well as certain forms of physical pain. Resting there deep inside, beyond fascia, the muscle could enable a user to draw one's knees up toward their chest, or to lean across a table and kiss a companion, or, in a broader and more clinical sense, to achieve certain qualities of bending and reaching. And yet the muscle had no name, the pain, no name, the symptoms too unnamed, the achievements attributed to the rest of the body. Without the development of this muscle, a body would be lacking, deformed, handicapped. But without a name, these afflictions, inconsistencies, abilities, whatever one chose to call them, remained a series of obscene mistakes, attributed to other parts of the body, issues of will or psychology, or what have you.

And so it was that between us we embarked on a colossal attempt to write this phenomenon, not in the scientific sense, not to prove or disprove a single thing, nor in the critical sense, to discover or pursue knowledge. We set about, in other words, to animate the creative force of her discovery, to give the invisibility of what she'd found life through metaphor, language, the slippage of meanings into wonder, sense replaced by tune.

All this as context to describe to you a single moment. Breakfasting at a French café I quite admire (this being said because the owner saw immediately that what was lacking in a city filled to the brim with French cafés and cuisine was a pleasant, easy, countryside version of a stopping-off place, a place for respite). The owner and I were on very good terms. Our table filled with black cherry preserves, croissants, café au lait, sitting as we had every Sunday in months of Sundays, her telling me more and more, me absorbing like some flesh machine. And she draws one leg up and crosses it over the other, the simplest gesture in the world, and the sun, and the smallness of the table, her lips, a thudding at my temples, my hand at her jaw, my torso leaning to the idea, to her, to it, the word appeared before me as her face appeared before me: *unentschieden*, undecided, floating, untethered. Its roots, *to do*. And more; in Yiddish, the word takes on the body in this state.

Do you see?

25

3. Trompe l'oeil

The city's Destination Sky Planetarium gave a laser-light show every Thursday and Friday night. The show included the music of Pink Floyd—*Dark Side of the Moon*—and the audience was mostly made up of young teenagers. On these nights the planetarium lost its science and gave way to sweat and the movement of hands and lips sunk down low in theater seats. Constellations and galaxies surrendered to configurations made of neon colored light, geometric patterns that could, through other means, translate into math equations. Music that failed to narrate and yet fully described. Eyes did not study, but were stoned, glassy gray and marble-like. The planetarium never filled on such occasions; however, it came as close to full as was possible, compared to any other time inside the bright domed world.

Destination Sky Planetarium had to be thoroughly cleaned every Saturday morning, as the teenagers left all manner of themselves behind, like sticky and worn cultural artifacts. Food, gum, cigarette butts. Condoms and rolling papers. Lip gloss and rubber bands. Plastic drink containers, soda cans, straws, and beer bottles that rolled to the center and rested there like tiny spaceships marooned and abandoned.

Ty Connor did the cleaning, and had been doing so for the last eight years. He'd learned the species in precise detail, he'd watched them gather there in the dark, recorded their behaviors, kept notes, formed hypotheses. And from the materials they left behind he'd build a kind of tiny city with an architecture of their leaving. His dining room table served as a sort of tableau of their existence, and the evidence of their presence emerged there like a sophisticated model of urban life circa the late 1990s, just before the millennium.

It had started simply enough. He'd found a lipstick and been mesmerized by the contraption, its easy rise and fall, its reminding him of gears or pistons or something mechanical. He'd pictured it immediately as some kind of tower in a building blue print, not unlike smoke stacks from the past, but in the newer, futuresque city it would hydraulically pump up and down, perhaps as a form of energy generation, perhaps as a mode of transport, similar to an elevator but more advanced. That had been the first piece, leading to the first drawings, and from there he began to collect other objects, and more and more of them, each with a distinctive purpose in the new city, the city born of youth, unthinking, disaffected, ignorant, and yet brilliant in its transitory existence. When he thought about them and the city evolving from them he was filled with awe, he saw the future bright and beautiful, a future that easily discarded morality and good citizenship in favor of an existence based on liminality and provisional presence, like television waves or information traveling by phone wire or electromagnetic light. It all made perfect sense to him, these beings, they were fully representative of a new order of existence, new cultures and architectures, space travel and cosmic weaponry fanning out into space. The vacant look in their eyes was not boredom or some residue of a Generation X apathy. It was the future dulling over ordinary vision, it was a blindness that led straight to insight.

No manner of event could draw him away from his obsession. By day he cleaned, and at night he worked on the city. Saturday evenings were a watershed of knowledge and a plethora of work—minute, painstaking labor that involved the careful consideration of objects, the fierce action of the imagination, steady hands and the will to create something from nothing. A bridge crossed a toxic waste site through a series of elevated tunnels made from cans and paper. Coke and Coke and Sprite and Diet Pepsi connected buildings like commercial passageways. Condoms stretched taut from pen to pen created great tents over business and technology centers. The tents had a dual purpose—to house the work within in a steady, temperature controlled environment, and to filter greenhouse gases through a complex bio-chemical procedure into hydrogen-oxygenated by-products, stored in heavy tanks made from Fruitopia bottles.

27

A feature that he was quite proud of was the garbage ventilation system, by which all means of waste was sucked down to the underneath of the city and processed into usable fuels. Every social space had great vents at its edges, and all airborne or material pollutants were simply sucked away, three times daily, eliminating trash, pollution, and even insects and rodents. After a terrible accident the first year of the program, grates had been installed so that small pets and children would not be accidentally removed from the socius. Since then the city had only increased in sheen and beauty. Ty had many notes, drawings and plans detailing systems such as these, and at times, just before sleep, he envisioned that his notebooks would someday be discovered and marveled at. Surely he was a mind ahead of his time.

28

Within these emotions and daily activities it happened one Saturday morning that Ty ran across an arm with his plastic-gloved hand down under one of the Destination Sky Planetarium seats. At first he though it was a baguette, since he'd found one with some molding brie cheese and an empty wine bottle once, then he thought it might be some kind of gag, a joke, a summer sausage, a stuffed pantyhose, something. But it was an arm. A human arm. Bodiless. The hand was intact, stiff and clawing and white. His breath jack-knifed in his lungs and his eyes bulged and watered in their sockets and his mind raced, what what what the fuck? And even as he held the lifeless thing in his plastic-gloved hand he couldn't get his brain to contain it, to lock on to it in the normal way, he just stood there like a great stuffed and thick beast, unable to move or speak or stop looking at it gesturing like that at him. It was stiff and heavy, and his own arm and hand began to stiffen and become heavy, as when a limb goes to sleep, or the brain forgets its body.

Some part of his mind very far away had a long conversation about turning the arm in to the authorities but he found himself putting it in the bag he saved for objects to take home with him instead. The rest of that day was awkward and herky-jerky. He spilled chlorine bleach all over the seats in the front row and the smell of a swimming pool on overload filled the Destination Sky Planetarium, nauseating and ice pick at the temple hard.

That night he did not work on the city at all. He drank three-quarters of a bottle of Jack Daniel's and fell asleep on the living room floor, the thick shag carpet tickling the very edges of his ears and fingers.

In the night strange visions made a fist of his brain, twisting his thoughts toward the obvious. His city was inorganic, artificial in every sense, and he'd failed to notice it at all. He'd made no attempt to render nature. He'd constructed no versions of trees, water, sky or any of the elements that make up a world. He'd concentrated solely on the artifice, the built environment, and the science to hold it up. The arm entered his dreams not as an arm, but as an argument, as a logic of the organic and the biological that roared in laughter at his simple-mindedness. It had a face and a mouth, and it cackled away at the little man who'd built a city of forms like a child with an erector set. In the face of the looming hand and arm he felt immature and stunted. Like a dwarf, an intellectual midget.

But when he awoke late the next morning he had not a hangover, but a clarity of vision as sharp as a diamond lodged in the center of a skull. He understood with full force the error he had made, with his little city on the table, with his lack of drive, with his life. He saw with bright white light that his entire existence had been leading up to a single moment, that he'd very nearly missed it, he'd nearly blinked and missed it, the way we often do in our lives, as we drone along in what's ordinary and familiar, we almost always miss the moment at hand, even when everything in the universe is pointing the way to the sight. He saw that his superficial efforts with refuse were the key, that his dream had opened his eyes, that ruin and decay were themselves the givers of life, the secret of the universe, the place from which all stars collapse and all systems tower and all logic gets born.

He'd simply mistaken the act for the thing itself.

The day he laid himself down on the dining room table alongside the new city he thought of all the teenagers in the Destination Sky Planetarium coupling and seething, and he rested the arm, slightly blue and stiff, in the crux of his arm, cradling it in a way, and he closed his eyes to the world and readied himself for, not sleep, but alchemy, the shifting of molecules, the transmutation from solid to another form, from metal to gold, or liquid, or the speed of light itself.

4. Truth is for Poets

"You know, he really does drive me fucking nuts sometimes."

"Who does?"

"What?"

"Nuts. Who drives you nuts? I mean, who doesn't drive you nuts is probably a better question, but who were you speaking of just now?"

"Oh. Blake. He was at the house last night for Kira's birthday."

"Did he do something, or is this just your usual malaise at humankind?"

"He did that thing I told you about that I hate. Again."

"Oh. *That* thing. What the fuck are you talking about? Could you be a bit more precise?"

"That thing where he turns everything into this gigantic, prophetic *moment*—like he alone saw something great and all of us chuckleheads missed it. Remember when we were talking about him and I said he does that, and you said you thought it was because he was a poet? Right on the goddamn money. I hate that shit. Makes me want to clock him one. Every time."

"Well, what was it this time?"

"It's after dinner, after cake, the celebration has sort of petered out, and the adults, me, Eric, and Blake are drinking brandy. Kira decides she's in one of her singing, theatrical moods, and she proceeds to go through half the score to *Mary Poppins*."

"That's cute. That's really fucking adorable. So how does Blake come in?"

"Yeah, it's cute. It might even be fucking adorable. But she's nothing special. I mean, I love her like nobody's business, don't get me wrong, but she's just a kid, you know? She's your average, interesting, creative kid going through average kid things. It's no big deal. I mean, he doesn't have to live with her. He doesn't go through any hell with her. She never says things to him like I hate you and I hope you are consumed by rats when you tell her she can't do something."

"You sound kind of...worked up. What the hell happened?"

"Nothing. I mean, nothing that night."

"So what are you so fucking hyped up about?"

"It was the next day. A friend of mine had lunch with him, and he proceeds to tell this enigmatic and big-as-a-cinema-close-up story of the little angel daughter singing the score to *Mary Poppins*. Only in *his* version it's all a thousand times more dramatic. He's got her waltzing into the dining room in a costume, waving her arms around and acting out the part, a perfect little smudge of soot on her nose. He's got her achieving a perfect cockney accent on her chim chimineys and supercalifragilistic-expialidociouses. I mean Christ. He even told the guy that she took off a little hat and circulated it among us for loose change before she magically retired upstairs to her bedroom."

"That's a great story...don't you think..."

"Sure it's a great fucking story. Except what really happened is she was trying to weasel her way out of bedtime any way she could, which is one of her newest tricks. She may have been charming the pants off of him, but she was pissing us off, and we'd been having to deal with trying to get her to go to bed before midnight for months."

"So?"

"So he goes out and tells everyone this magical story of the beautiful little princess girl captivating her audience."

"So?"

"So it just pisses me off, is all. He should have his own goddamn kid. Then we'd see how *poetic* his moments are."

"You sound like you resent him or something. I mean, he *is* a poet. That's what he does. That's *all* he does."

"Well maybe I just wish he'd get his own material, use his own goddamn life for fucking little moments of beauty and light. Maybe I wish he'd get a life and have to deal with the shitty parts like the rest of us."

"Maybe you wish you were him."

"Fuck that. I'd rather eat glass, honestly. When you walk around with rose-colored glasses you miss most of life. Most of life is difficult, painful, even boring. But it's real. Real relationships, real experiences. You know what I'm saying?"

"Sure. You're saying art is outside of life, and that the way he lives in his art pisses you off. Like he's deluded or blinded somehow. Like he borrows other people's experiences without their permission."

"That's what I'm saying."

"I see what you mean."

"He'll do it again, I know he will. It's his only modus operandi. Fucking poets. You wait and see, he'll get you too."

An American Couple

Thirty days has September. Living in thirty day increments, divided by hours and tasks and errands. Calendars that keep us putting the same two shoes on each day, putting gas in the car, clocks that keep us turning the handle of a doorknob. Look, it is time for the nightly news, then dinner. Oh, the mail is coming in about half an hour. Or: I feel the desire to have a glass of red wine, sit on the back porch. Take my shoes off. It is obviously around five o'clock. At six I will experience the uncontrollable urge to see Peter Jennings' face.

Good Evening
But First, A Look At Today's Top Stories
E-N-A-B-L-E-R

I go around in the house or out of it in the same way. I make goals and I have too much drive, so I often achieve things. I am intolerable in waves, a helluvah person to live with in that way. I think of this as monstrous, but I do not succumb to martyrdom or victimhood; I plow forward, each success larger than the last, huge, garish. I eat what I want when I want, it doesn't bother me to be heavy or thin, I can drink anyone under the table or not drink at

all. I can reinvent myself in one week by getting a haircut.
I can quit one life and construct another in three months.
If I want to do nothing for thirty days it would not reflect
badly on me. Instead of sloth, it would take on the form
of necessary rest, and the next thing I put my mind to I
would achieve doubly well. I am sickening.

Try to give me a Christmas present. Try, I dare you.

He goes downstairs in the basement and pretends to
do laundry. He brought three jugs of wine in through the
back door straight downstairs to avoid coming into the
shared part of the house. He opens one. He turns on some
music down there, also the dryer. He drinks straight from
the bottle in huge gulps, then pours himself a glass. There
is a sofa chair down there from their past. He sits in it, a
single light bulb illuminating things. It is not as if he needs
to hide anything. He could enact the very same movements sitting next to her on the couch, watching the
nightly news, simple as pie. He's down there for him, he
needs the secrecy, he's constructed the secret in spite of
her. There are bottles everywhere. Sometimes she picks
them up, sometimes not, sometimes they talk about it,
you wouldn't believe how well she understands it all, an
artist like him, she understands it all better than anyone
else in the universe. When she was younger she was sent
to a recovery clinic for heroin addiction. Becoming a writer
saved her life. Can't beat that, now can you. You can never
beat that.

There are paintings and paint and brushes and smells
of his life down there in the basement too. That's where
he works. They converted the basement into a studio. She
suggested it. You wouldn't believe how much she believes
in him. When he told her he wanted to paint, years ago,
she was like a snake, all spine and nerve, ready for action. That very Christmas, she bought two huge easels.
All the brushes he could want. Paint. Canvas. That year
they rebuilt what is meant to be under the house into what
is not. He sits down there alone in the sofa chair from
their past and tears well up in his eyes. He can hear her

footsteps upstairs. She knows he is down there, knows what he is doing, probably even knows he is crying a bit. She'll only know more and more.

The internet makes life into little boxes, little electronic exchanges. Once or twice a month I gravitate toward a social encounter. Drinks with a woman friend. It is a kind of relief, a way to keep things going, to feel a rhythm. I don't like people otherwise. Screen-life simplifies social pressures.

To: L

From: L

Subject: Tequila

We drink tequila shots on a Thursday evening at five and it is warm and she smiles and laughs. We are colleagues. Our names are alike. I like to watch her face. I like to listen to her talk about her life. She is ten years older than I am. She is beautiful, in that way that women get, when they have moved beyond wanting things they will never get and have gotten things they never wanted. A kind of calm. Her discipline is psychology. Mine is literature. The two disciplines swim toward each other, merge, then divide like cells. Women professionals. Salt and lemon; liquid.

She tells me she had a fight with her husband. She was talking about the dream she has of quitting teaching and owning a horse ranch eventually. For the first time in twenty years he said, I don't share your dream, I don't want to live that life. While she was talking I had these thoughts that were interrupting my listening like: she is so pretty. She doesn't look like an academic. Those boys at the table next to us have been looking at her all night. What are they, about twenty-one? Drinking age? Little shits. She tells me about the last conference she was at and the Irish bartender. She ordered and ordered drinks until it was a code between them, until it was last call, until it was closing time, until they walked and walked all night together on an East Coast. It was a long night in the life of a woman. Just walking. Like that. A year later

35

she goes to the same conference and he is the same bartender. First he doesn't see her. Then, through a crowd of
yuppies and people ten, fifteen, twenty years younger
than her, a drop-dead smile creeping up the side of his
face shows his memory. He brings her a drink she has not
yet ordered. Her heart beats past rupture. She tells me
and tells me. It is just like a movie. I know not to ask too
many questions. Her cheeks blush and mine do too. We
drink and drink. We laugh until we cry.

Later we are tanked. The stories between us get more
serious. She tells me about her daughter's leg, about a
year of torture and pain waiting for a child to be well. I
tell her about my family. I tell her how my father, who
was an abusive prick, drowned in the ocean, and how I
pulled him out and resuscitated him. It's a hard story to
tell, people's eyes get big and they seem to not believe it
as I tell it. The older I get, the less I can bear telling it. She
asks me why I did that. I say I don't know. It is true, I
don't. She asks me if I thought about letting him die there,
on the beach. I say I wasn't thinking.

On the drive home we are still laughing about this,
that, and the other. We are acting as if everything is fine.
We are behaving as if we are two women riding randomly
and with ease in a car, without any job or daughter or
husband, with nothing but sky.

He has a show of his work. A one man show, entitled,
"I am Cross With God: Intimate Portraits." It is a series of
abstract portraits, faces coming apart, eyes, mouths bleeding into form and color. Screams and smiles indistinguishable from one another. At the opening, someone asks him,
are the images meant to look so tortured? He has had
seven glasses of wine in less than half an hour. He looks
at the person asking the question as if their face is about
to float off into space. He says, tortured? The person asking the question elaborates. They all look like they are in
pain. He says, the next time you are in a passionate kiss
with someone, open your eyes. Think about what their
face looks like. That close. That familiar. So familiar you

can't bear it. Then he walks off, taking one of the bottles from the table with him.

One of the students I am fond of comes to my office the last day of the term. She has this black leather small suitcase-type thing with her. It is around five o'clock; traffic will be accumulating soon. She closes the door and opens the black leather suitcase. Inside she has the makings for gin and tonics, complete with lime and a small knife. We laugh and laugh. We drink for hours and hours. We talk until the talk becomes dizzy and repetitive, we are telling each other stories about young women and their wild ways, the girls we were. We laugh and tell these stories until her boyfriend knocks on the door and tells her he has been looking for her for hours, her kids were waiting for her to pick them up at the wrestling match, what got into her, anyway? We're tanked and so laugh some more, our faces red and our eyes puffy. We must look cute, because he laughs too, then we all sit back down and wait for me to be able to drive home.

I commute. I like to think and talk to myself on the drive. On the way home that night I think what a strange and sweet gift it was, that young woman coming by like that, with a little gin picnic in a black leather suitcase. Sexy. Playful. It tickles me to no end, the way I would have never guessed something like that would happen. I laugh out loud. It's this: I hate teaching, in a general sense. A T-shirt the same student gives me:

Oh My God; I forgot to Have Children

He is in his studio. It is night. He has yet to turn any lights on. In the dark there the images come from nothing. Surfacing in the dimness, then receding. Like memory. Like love. They haunt him. He sits alone alone alone and relief like that.

Sometimes I follow him. He says, I'm going to pick up some steaks for dinner. I say OK without looking up from my work or the TV or whatever. But I watch him out of the corner of my eye. Since he is in the pick-up, I can get in the Toyota, start it, and rev around the corner before he makes it to the corner where he turns to go to the market. So I wait to make the bend until I see his tail-lights disappear. I know where he is going. He is going to the bar two blocks up from the market. From my car across the road and up some I can see into the bar. I can see him ordering. I can see him slamming one drink, sometimes two. Before he pays I leave. Beat him home. Remake my body on the couch or in the chair without skipping a beat.

Other times he goes to a liquor store if he can make it before five o'clock. He buys a bottle of wine and sits in his car and drinks it. I watch the back of his head rock back. Rock back. Rock back. I cry. It is the deepest compassion I will ever feel in my life. It is a deeper compassion and sadness than I felt when my daughter died. It is a compassion that could drown us.

He times his market trips around happy hour and closing time at the liquor store. It is lucky that dinner falls when it does in the course of a day. It is astonishingly lucky. It is precise in its ridiculousness.

I am teaching the story of the bourgeois couple for the hundredth time. Don DeLillo this time. The couple rises with the action. The couple falls into itself. The man is running. The woman is dying. Isn't she beautiful. Isn't the humor of the book fantastic when, on page such and such, there is a parody of sexual fantasies and how we have lost touch with eroticism.

A critic on his work: "The dissolutions of the face bring us to that place where signification breaks down, where word, image, sign, are released from systems and set adrift. The face loses itself to the chaos of life." He reads it and then burns it and then drinks martinis from an old tin coffee can. He can see a version of his face reflected in the tin; disfigured.

A different colleague. A sociologist. We both have blonde hair. When we enter the bar all the heads turn. Like we are a Scandinavian Front or something. We begin to order Cosmopolitans because the kind of men who come to this bar are suits and smoke cigars and the kind of women who come to this bar are not like us either. The waitress talks us into Lemondrops—a specialty of this kind of bar. They taste mildly of cough syrup and heavy doses of vitamin C. We laugh and laugh. Isn't it funny? We will avoid colds, we will build up our immune systems, the syrupy stuff will coat our insides like thick medicine. She was married once eight years ago. Since then she has had two affairs. One man turned out to be a junkie and fucked one of her students, then they left the state together in a van. Just so sixties. Just like that. The other man was one of our colleagues. He didn't like sex. Or just didn't need it. Or just didn't care. They enjoyed each other's company until it hurt too much.

39

I don't know why I need this. To be alone with these women. These professional women. I don't know why it feels so good to laugh so hard at nothing, at the cusp of forty, or beyond, or anything in between. I don't know why their relationships work, nor do I know why they don't. I know nothing about anything. The sociologist and the psychologist and the English professor—all of them agree. Between us we know absolutely nothing about anything. It is so fucking funny I feel as if I could die laughing.

He thinks: I could leave the country. I could not need to contribute to the scheme of things and I could stop pretending to like Mingus and Nina Simone. If I close my eyes, I could be in another country and women who are completely uneducated and adoring might come sit with me and stare out at the ocean, or at the wind in the palms, or at nothing at all. But that's the gut of it, isn't it. That they'd keep on not knowing and not knowing him at all, and at first it would be heaven; then not. Then her image would come back to him as it always does, her image that haunts him in the dark of his mind, the dark of his skull, the goddamn insides of his eyeballs, her smart, wickedly intelligent, horrible self. He turns the radio on and roughly steers the station to classic rock. She is right, it's pretty bad. He turns it up and up. He grinds his teeth. He tries to engage in conversation with the noise, the past, the sounds coming out at him. If they would just shut up long enough for him to say the things he needs to say.

Let it be.

Rock Steady.

Paranoia.

The girl with far away eyes.

Stop making sense.

40   He turns the sound all the way up, closes his eyes, drives like that for about ten seconds. Ten seconds of life. He is salivating. The rest of the day will go exactly as the ones before it. His body moves toward liquid, a twitch of fin, a curl of water around rocks, natural, beautiful, serene.

We've made Xerox copies of every other couple in America. We have fucked other people. We have denied it, then tried to act it out as crisis. Our families are exactly as fucked up as everyone's. My tyrannical father drowned in the ocean. His cold-hearted mother eaten by cancer. In place of children we carry a dead child living between us. I get good jobs. We inhabit houses. Rent apartments. Travel. Fights. Depressions. Recoveries. Money moving between two people like an ironic green hand fan. Perpetual spasms of life coming and going. A relationship more and more unknowable. More and more written. More and more painted.

Sometimes I drive to his studio when I am certain he will not be there. I go very early in the morning, and it is like Christmas, exactly like that, because I open the door and it is as if treasure and shine and light fill the room. Other times I go late at night, late enough so as to approach morning, after I have been out with one of my women friends, after we have laughed and laughed, or talked our relationships to death, or come to vast new conclusions about nothing and our know-nothingness. In that place not dusk and not dawn, neither light nor dark, I'm weightless as a shadow. I'm invisible. I'm not any body's deadening effect, I'm not driven and successful, I'm not loathing a self either. I'm just a woman in a room with hundreds of paintings I will never know. I'm there. Like that. Unreflected. Without me.

41

Shadow Boxing

Jesus Complex

Guy busts into the diner I'm in and blares out, there's
a woman on top of the First National Bank tower, somebody get some help! I'm scraping the inside of my coffee
cup with a spoon. The circles grate; people in booths cringe
and look at me. I take my time turning around. She doesn't
need any help, I say. He's flapping and squawking—but
she's naked! And she's up there, Christ, what if she jumps?
I continue my unbearable stirring. People have turned
their attention to us, a little drama for lunch. I stop stirring to say, that ain't why she's up there, and then I begin
again. I don't even look at him. I can hear his agitation as
he lurches over to me, in my face, how the hell do you
know? He's exasperated. Try being married to her for a
few years, I think. Try living that life for one fucking day.
Try, you pathetic little noble-hearted cretin. I finally turn
and look at him. I tell him. I know because I've been up
there. Not just this time. Hundreds of times. And buddy,
I can tell you, this is the last time. I ain't going up there
anymore. In Cleveland it was the pump station, in Bos-
ton the tower in Harvard Square, in Lubbock the Buddy

Holly statue—which, mind you, is only 10 feet off the ground. No sir, this is it. I'm not going up any more. I drink the whole cup down in one gesture, like all the years settling into one, fine, luke-warm, caffeinated beverage.

He's not satisfied. Look mister, he says, I don't care if she is your wife—x wife, I correct him—whatever, x wife, she's in trouble and somebody needs to help. We can't just stand by and let—I laugh and snort. For your information, I was just up there half an hour ago. Talking her down on a goddamn walkie-talkie the entire way up. Instructions from people I don't know accompanying me. You know, strangers are FULL to the brim with advice until the moment of crisis itself, then they stand there with their goddamn mouths open like bloated and paralyzed fish. I get up there, again, for the I-don't-know-how-manieth time, and she is cool as a fucking cucumber. First thing she says to me is what the hell are you doing here? Couldn't they find somebody more suitable? Christ. More suitable. Just for the sake of argument, I say, since we've been through this before and I feel a certain familiarity, I say, what do you mean by "suitable?" Do you mean you'd prefer a guy in a suit? I laugh. She doesn't. Someone more dramatic, less, I don't know, ordinary. I look down at the tar on the roof there. Old baseballs, wadded up paper, wire, weird stuff up there. And I say Lily, I think they assume we have a common history. She looks off and says well THEY should have considered the full ramifications of that. I say jeez, are things really THAT BAD that you have to do stuff like this for the rest of your life? Wasn't it enough for us to go busto? When I say THAT BAD I make the mistake of waving my arms around. She counters by waving her arms around wildly and saying as a matter of fact, THINGS have never been BETTER. Throws one leg over the edge in this kind of epileptic like fit. That was the whole marriage—one leg over the edge.

From the ground you see a helpless naked woman lurching and retracting.

I then make mistake number two. I say, well, you look great. She says you motherfucker. She starts cursing so

43

YUKNAVITCH

Lidia

hard spit flies out of her mouth and her hair rages around like crazy. She says you are the most predictable being on the planet. You are like Tupperware. Then she makes obscene flailings with the other leg and falls in a thump there so she's sort of sitting on the edge. My heart is jack-knifing in my lungs; old feeling. I move toward her out of instinct, hell, anyone would. I take a moment of comfort in that notion—anyone in their right mind would move toward a naked woman on top of a roof if she got too close to the edge. How sane. How normal. She darts a you're dead look at me and says look, don't be a pathetic ass. You can't get me down from here. You can't get me to put my clothes back on. You couldn't get me to be a wife. If you try to grab me I'll just divorce you in a more POTENT and PERMANENT way, if you know what I mean. Got it?

44

I just stand there staring at nothing. This is a feeling so familiar I can't recognize it. Me with my hands dangling from the ends of my know-nothing arms like a jerk. Me looking at the ground, no matter where I am in my life, no matter what successes, failures, confidence, not. We freeze there like that for a long minute. The image is striking. She calms in that moment. A light breeze joins us. You know what's extraordinary she says. What, I say. You can see flight from the top. Yet another in a series of completely incomprehensible statements out of the mouth of what always appeared to be a normal, beautiful, intelligent woman. I respond, who knows why. Maybe it's inevitable. What are you talking about? I'm tired. I don't want to listen to her nonsense anymore. I am more tired than I have been in my entire life. We're not even together anymore, and won't be, I could remarry, I could have a thousand different lives in a thousand different worlds, and we'd still meet here, like this, in this way. Birds, she says. From up here, you see them from the top, not the belly side. See their backs, the top side of their wingedness. And she holds her hands and arms out like wings. For an instant I think, my God, she is as beautiful as ever, she is so crazy and angry and interesting that she is larger than life, and next I snap out of it, I think this is it, this is really it, she's changed, she's different somehow, if the wind blows she'll lose her balance, and I screech LILY DON'T—FOR CHRIST'S SAKE DON'T—

She says don't be an ass. I'm not a bird.

So I'm going to sit here, and I'm going to drink this coffee, and when I'm done I'm going to walk out of here and I'm never going to see her again. I'm a young man. I've got a life, pal. You wanna save her? Knock yourself out.

Second Coming

Why did she do it? I would say that she did it out of love, for me. But not your ordinary kind of love. She is a very selfish person. She is probably the most selfish person I know. For example, I don't know how cognizant she was of the depth of despair I had experienced in those years, its specificity. I don't think she understood what I was going through at all. But she always had a kind of primal intuition about pain in general. Even when she was a kid, if someone was suffering in some way, she'd run in and try to save them. Injured people, cats, dogs, moths caught inside trying to get out, someone crying or just lonely, she even designed a sling for a broken branch of an old oak tree once. And if you were to look her in the eye and ask her for something, I mean even if a stranger did, I don't think there is anything she wouldn't do for you if you asked her to. Bums had big nights because of her. Once she helped an old crazy guy get loose out of a side gate to St. Mary's. So when I asked her it had a logic.

The day I asked her I hadn't an idea in hell where to get the equipment I needed. I had a book with directions regarding the proper procedure and the kinds of things people used. Plastic cooking basters, syringes, tubing, rubber, oil. She had several different size syringes. I don't know why I didn't think more about that. I only felt lucky not to have to go and purchase one. She had one that was the perfect size. We did end up having to buy this plastic cap gizmo with a hole in it that fit over my cervix. To contain the little devils and increase the chance of success.

45

Another item that turned out to be incredibly useful was her vibrator. When she asked me if I wanted to use one to get off first I just looked at her blankly. She said don't you know what a vibrator is? I didn't. This tickled her. She said that figures, the younger sister has to coach the older, wiser sister on the proper use of a sex toy. We laughed. When she brought it out I blushed. I asked her what you were supposed to do with the thing, stick it up there, or what, and then we laughed some more, and she told me when the time came she'd show me.

There are several strategies a woman can use to increase the chances of her success if she is going it alone. I didn't have the money to set up a procedure at the clinic, so I was giving it my best shot. One thing that helps is to stimulate the organs, as during intercourse. The increased mucous and swelling prime the vagina and cervix. You know, like motor oil. Another thing that helps is to get into a position in which your feet are higher than your ass. Like Yoga. Makes sense, doesn't it. A warm water solution in a cup helps the semen collect in such a way so that it sucks up into the syringe well, and so that it disperses evenly into the vagina. Once the semen is inside, it also helps to remain in that reversed incline position so that the little fellas don't leak back out. Details.

My sister's husband was in the bedroom, watching TV. I was propped up in a reverse incline on the couch in the living room. She'd bought this great deep red blanket and I was nestled down into it. She'd arranged candles, incense, and flowers everywhere; the room was heavenly. She'd convinced me to take all of my clothes off. I remember when I said, I just need to be naked from the waist down, she said, you may as well get some pleasure out of this, right? Seemed true. Celtic harp music made the room a little dizzy, or else it was the red wine she convinced me to drink. My skin was warm. Sweat was forming underneath my breasts and between my legs. She brought the vibrator to my hands, and turned it on. I didn't really know what to do with it, so she guided my hands. At first she touched my lips with it, and I had a deep and to the bone tingling sensation all throughout my body. She then pushed it down to where my clitoris was for a few seconds, and my entire body spasmed; then she withdrew it quickly and touched it to my breasts, my nipples, one at a time. She then moved it down again, and at a certain point she let go so that I was guiding the movement. My eyes were closed, my hands were alive. I was breathing very hard. At a certain point I opened my eyes; they felt puffy, my lips too, and I looked at her. I was rocking my hips and moving my hands and the scent of my cunt rose up between us as I was looking at her. She was smiling and staring at my cunt, and I liked her staring there, then she looked into my eyes, and I felt an overwhelming desire for her to say something, and she said, touch your tits with it again, and I did that, and then she said, now put it back in your pussy, move it around…and then I closed my eyes again. I think I heard her whisper that she was going to the bedroom and that I should keep doing it.

While she was there I heard moaning, and I came shortly after that. When she came back she had the cup full and I was wet and flushed and filled with my own desire turned in on itself.

She nestled herself between my legs in a kind of kneeling position. She filled the syringe without my noticing. She told me to close my eyes. She tickled an imaginary line down my body from my breasts to my cunt with her finger. Then two of her fingers entered me, and she rubbed around in circles. She said, can you hold your lips apart, wide apart? I did. My cunt throbbed so hard I thought it must appear to her like a mouth opening and closing. I closed my eyes again. I felt her fingers there still, and then I felt the syringe enter me, but she had her fingers around it in such a way so that it was unbearably gentle. I bit the inside of my cheek. I felt the overwhelming urge to beg her to do it harder, then I felt crazy, then I shot that thought out of my brain. I did not feel her expel the syringe but she was moving her hand and the syringe in and out when she did it.

When I opened my eyes I had tears, I saw her head and face between my legs, the light of her blonde hair, the heat of her skin, her mouth, open.

Later we all had dessert and watched a movie.

I remember the day she was born.

The Eleventh Commandment

To this day I don't know why she hung out with me. I was pitiful. Sickly, pale, booger-picking. Braces. Matted hair that argued with itself like crazy. The works. You can imagine; I was the kind that sat in those cement tunnels by myself all during recess because nobody would play with me. I was the kid that wet my pants during social studies in sixth grade. You heard right. Sixth grade. I had already developed several neuroses. I had the stress of a forty-eight-year-old man. Are you getting the picture? Sure you are, because everyone had a kid like me around.

The first time I met her she came into one of those tunnels and sat beside me without saying a word. For the whole recess period. I didn't say a word either. I was scared but thankful, in a weird sort of way. She didn't even look at me.

The next day she got in there with me again, and toward the end of the 45 minutes she said, Chris Backstrom has hair around his pecker. That's all. Then the bell rang and she ran out, and I sat there for awhile longer considering this. Chris Backstrom had blonde hair, so I was trying to picture blonde hair growing in beautiful curls around his penis. I shuddered and thought I might vomit. Then I got a splitting headache. I kept checking to see if my nose was bleeding. By the time I made it back to the classroom I was near fainting with pain, and they sent me to the nurse's office. After some time my mother picked me up and I went home. She was very angry.

About a week later she came in there and said she wanted to show me something. She said it was very unique, and that never in a million years would I get the chance again. Then she asked me if I wanted to see. My mouth was filled with saliva and my palms were sweaty. I felt an uncontrollable urge to pick my nose, then I thought I might have to pee. I said yes in a wobbly little fairy voice. I thought I might have gone cross-eyed there for a second.

She lifted up her skirt and she pulled her panties down. This smell filled the concrete tunnel and it was good, but it was also terrifying, and I thought I could somehow taste it.

When I look back I think of how she saved my life that day.

Her pussy had little red hairs on it and she said, see, this is very rare. And she took my hand and we pet her together.

49

Later she coaxed me out of the tunnel and we walked around to the far end of the field where the goal posts were. Some boys were playing soccer and as true as life the ball ended up clocking me upside the head. My face turned more red than is humanly possible, a stinging animated my skin. My skull throbbed like an over-ripe fruit, I felt certain my head was nearing rupture. I thought about it exploding there on the field, and how everyone would laugh, and then they would stare, stunned, realizing the death laid bare before them, the dull head of a boy in pieces at their feet.

The boys came toward us, and then I pictured another death, death by pulverization, death by them gnashing their teeth and cannibalizing me on the field. Food. I felt like too-white food.

As was the case during most of grade school, they began to taunt me, sort of ignoring her, drawing a tight circle around me until it felt as if the oxygen was being sucked right out of my lungs. One of the leaders of the pack came up and over me, his great mouth opening and closing, his teeth drawing nearer, he was yelling, his spit was evident, his breath hot and burning on my face, his chest puffing out and his hand drawing back and his body moving with the weight of an animal on me.

Then she was there, between us, and she was saying the most incomprehensible sentence, like a new language or something, stopping the turning of the world. She said, you know about the eleventh commandment, don't you, and at first the guy tried to shove her aside and then she shouldered her way back in, since, after all, she was taller than him, as is often the case at that age.

Somehow she got his attention. She got all the attention.

She said it again. The eleventh commandment. It's in this secret book that someone found in a clay pot. They kept all the secret stuff out of the real Bible because it scared people too much and it was too difficult for most people to understand. You had to have intelligence, but you also had to have imagination, and most people barely have the one and have none of the other. Like you chuckleheads.

The story was mesmerizing enough that they let go of her insult.

In the secret books there is an extra commandment, and it's bigger and more serious than all the other ones, because it includes what will happen to you if you sin against it. Some boy to the side yelled out, you're full of shit, there's only one Bible, shut up you stupid bitch. She kept talking on her way over to him until her words were breath-close to his face. The reason you don't know about it, dumbfuck, is that no one thinks you are smart enough to get it. They don't let just anyone in on it. You have to prove yourself. You have to show them you are worthy, mature, that you can handle it. But I'm gonna tell you because you're all too stupid to get that far, and I think it might save you some trouble later in life.

I don't know how girls like that get the power to lead people. I don't know what it was about her—she wasn't pretty like the popular girls, and she wasn't athletic enough for that to work. It was more like she had this little bit of craziness that made people scared of her, but like all violence, it also made you want to look, listen.

Some other schmuck called out, well how the hell did YOU hear about it? And she very calmly explained, Mary Shelley came to me in a dream and told me about it. The same guy said who the hell is that? She got a look on her face like she was speaking to chimps. She took a deep breath and said, Mary Shelley, shit for brains, wrote *Frankenstein*, the greatest book of all time. If any of you clowns knew how to fucking read you'd know that.

Then she made her way back over to me, me standing in a puddle of fear, airless, weightless, dizzy, me already having surrendered, already having left my body to be beaten, to enjoy the beating. She stood very near me and told the story of the eleventh commandment.

There was this leper that was friends with Jesus. Everybody was grossed out by him on account of his nastiness, his skin was all gray and pussy and it had these horrible open wounds and shit on it. He was actually a pretty nice guy, but no one wanted to go near him, and since most humans are stupid asses, they translated their disgust of his skin to him, and that meant that he was evil, dangerous, deviant and shitty in the worst of ways. But Jesus, being a smart motherfucker, really liked him. He even thought the skin thing was interesting, after all, it made him unique and closer to God from all that suffering. Besides, he'd played chess with him and had great philosophical conversations with him and shared scotch with him so he knew he was phat. It was just the losers in the town that didn't know shit.

So one day this kid passed by the house that the leper lived in and he peeked inside the window and saw the leper and Jesus fucking (at this point the crowd of boys began to hurl obscenities at her in disbelief). I know, the town reacted exactly like you morons, they were saying shit exactly like you are. But the fact was, Jesus and the leper were fucking. So the town, like you assholes, decided that Jesus was either posessed by the leper-devil or under some kind of leper-devil hex, and they set out to save him.

Though I wasn't fully conscious of it, the air began to enter my insectually small lungs again, bit by bit, and it is

51

possible that I could feel my own hands dangling from their arms again.

Since they were stupid, their plan was stupid. They decided that they would wait for the leper to go to sleep and then they would burn him and his house to ash. Of course Jesus ended up in bed with him that night, and they burned 'em both to ash.

God was pretty pissed, as you can imagine, and the next morning he cracked the sky open with lightning and put out the eye of the sun and threw down a rock slab with its own commandment on it that said: Thou shalt for the rest of time be stricken with disease when thou claps eyes upon the uncanny, and the second they read the thing all their peckers turned black and the pain of acid on flesh shriveled 'em up and after a week or so their dicks dropped off. And that's what happens to anyone who witnesses the uncanny without knowing what it means, without understanding they are looking at a fucking miracle.

It was the strangest story we'd ever heard, strange because we didn't know what "uncanny" meant, but also because she did, and because our little dicks were getting hard from this tall woman telling us a story like that. Strange because we hated anything about homos and strange because half of us were, or were on our way to becoming, homos.

It's not like they couldn't have beaten the crap out of my sorry-ass anyway, or pushed her around, or any number of sadistic scenes, but somehow her story left this little path off of the field for us, and she walked it, and I followed her, and I got the impression that the waves would hold like that until the Romans turned to chase us, at which point they would be consumed by the sea, or perhaps just all of our ignorance drowning us out and away.

AGAINST INTERPRETATION

Cusp

This bed smells of my skin. If I roll from my back to my belly, sweat cools near my spine. If I close my eyes, I am like an animal up here in the heat and wood, baking in the daylight, my eyelids heavy, my thoughts slow and thudding. I am waiting for dark, for the release, for breathing to animate me. This room and everything in it brings me closer to myself: nocturnal.

From the frame of my attic window I have imagined the inside-out of this town. Its heat rising from dust and scrub and asphalt like pulse and blood and organs, its mindless longing for rain, its heart beating with dumb insistence. Outside of my room the world has expanded and contracted like the tight little fist of a child. Years have gone by. I used to think, who would want to live here, like this, some town at the edge of the storyline, the nightly news, never quite making it into the picture, its people peopling over geography somehow without evolution or design? Washed-up, dried out. There is a black and red sign over the door of the Texaco. It reads: "Texas, USA." No city. No need. That's the whole deal stuck up there on a piece of metal the size of a license plate. Like thought stopped for gas and didn't leave.

I remember the day I moved from my room downstairs to the attic. It had been my brother's. He'd gone to
college, I'd hit puberty, the two motions crossing paths
with fierce electricity. The white canopy bed of a girl died
that day, for I never went back. Through the alchemy of a
family I moved into the attic room of my brother. My first
day in the attic I felt the wooden walls close in around
me. It was as if a second body was there to hold me, and
the wood grain looked to me like dark warm skin. Like I
was walled in by a second skin.

Underneath the bed I found artifacts from my
brother's life. Empty bottles and broken glass, trash, foil,
used rubbers and tissues, tiny vials and a stretch of surgi-
cal tubing. I didn't find needles for a year, but it was not
for lack of looking. He'd shown me his world when I was
around ten, knowing I would be in love with it as I was
with all the moments he let me be in his attic, adoring
him, adoring the dark of the room, the rules broken, the
silence thick and almost unbearable, the smells I hadn't
names for, the dizzy swell of skin making sweat. But I did
find everything. A loose board in the wall, a stash I only
barely comprehended at the time. Wasn't I meant to find
it, to find it all? Wasn't I meant to identify the smell as sex
and move my body toward delivering itself? Wasn't I
meant to rise to the challenge, to prove my worth, to carry
on the weight of that room? Brother.

On my fourteenth birthday I got Jack Daniels from
my brother. He was home from college for the summer.
He gave it to me in secret, after dark, and we sat up in the
attic window that connected our lives and drank it until I
was bleary and swollen and unable to focus. At some point
after midnight we became heated and half-clothed. The
heat works on you like that. You shed layers like the skin
of a snake until the body can bear itself. My brother
brought the amber liquid to his face, took it, held it in his
mouth like that with his eyes closed.

"Well," he said, "it's almost here, huh?"

"You mean that," I said, gesturing out of the window
in the direction of the future to the place out there in the

dark where something foreign was emerging. It was a prison, or the idea of one, a place of curiosity and danger emerging in a town smothering a brother and a sister.

"Yeah, guess that will change things around here."

"It's the best thing that's ever happened to me in my sorry-ass little life."

He looked at me, I think he toasted me, and he said, "You'll get out soon enough. You'll see. When you get out, it's a whole new world, a new life."

"What if I don't get out?"

He laughed and laughed. "You? You were out the day you were born. You'll probably end up at Harvard or some fancy-ass shit. You've got brains."

"You've got brains too," I said, "that's how you got where you are." He snorted and downed his drink.

"Pour me another," and then, "you don't know what the fuck you're talking about."

"What do you mean?"

He looked at me a long time, as if he was judging my worthiness in this conversation. Finally he took a new sip and said, "Between you and me?"

"Sure."

"I dropped out."

"What the hell are you talking about?"

"I quit. I haven't been back for months. I've been working at a construction sight near my apartment and selling some shit on the side. It's not great, but it's a life. And I'm meeting people—important guys. Guys who are connected."

"Do you mean to say that you're telling them you are at college when in reality you are fucking conning them?"

"What's the con? I'm making a living on my own. I've got money. Sex. A job. Fixing any time I want. And like I said, I'm meeting some important people. The building we are working on right now is filled with money. Big opportunity. The guy behind the scenes is filthy rich. Had us up to his house in Dallas for a party. Wild, man. Chicks walking around with nothing but G-strings on, carrying mirrors of coke lines like platters at a restaurant. Pussy everywhere."

I looked down at my hands, then down some more, into my own lap, between my own legs, to that place not yet "pussy" but aching to be.

"What's the matter? Hasn't anyone ever said 'pussy' to you?"

I nodded but couldn't look up. My face was so hot I thought my head might explode. My hands made a pathetic cup between my legs. My lips puffed out like a kid's.

He laughed and laughed. "Grow up, baby. You'll learn the world of cunts and dicks soon enough." He poured me more to drink. "The whole world is one big fuck-fest. Forget this life. Forget families—mothers, fathers, school, jobs. There are only two kinds of winning, two ways of keeping score: bucks and fucks."

I tried to laugh knowingly, then drank, then just sat there. I admit it, I was in full awe. We sat in silence after that.

That birthday, from my parents, I received a set of all of Shakespeare's tragedies, used copies, but beautiful somehow. The covers were dark red and the writing was embossed. Inside the pages were as thin as moth's wings and I could picture them burning, one at a time, lifting themselves toward heaven. They didn't know me, but they knew I loved books more than just about anything in the world. They didn't know why. I loved books because my life there was killing me from the inside out. Every page filled with words was a chance for escape, a chance to suicide into a life where the brain was something more than a thick bundle of gray worms making the skull heavier, a place where the body lost its origins and confines and mutated endlessly. Whole worlds cupped between my hands. Truthfully, the only happiness I ever knew in that space came from between my legs, a bottle or a book, in those drunken places. Until the prison filled.

After he left, I thought about myself leaving, being at some college with ivy-covered walls, being in closed rooms with men who were spewing knowledge at me, writing papers that broke open dead worlds and constructed new architectures. After he left, I imagined living a double life in college, selling drugs, like him, fucking guys on the side for extra cash. A woman on the edge: Ophelia, rewriting her ending. After he left I cried. After he left my room I put my hand between my legs and rubbed so hard I thought I might bleed. Later I used a hairbrush to get at the deeper layers of what was inside me, to get it out, to make it alive and in the room with me, chaotic, heavy, wet and free.

Nights overtook me. Alone in the attic my hands dug and carried my sex into worlds of my own making. I brought my brother's face into the walls now and again, as if he was watching, or guarding, or lifting me into the darkness.

59

The day they lodged the last brick, stretched the last of the chain-link fencing, spiraled the final barbed loops over everything, that day sang like a fever in me. I knew my do-nothing life was about to be over. I knew like I knew the back of my hand that my dead and dull town had driven away like a herd of lost cows into dust and forever.

Two years of city council protests, petition signing and general small town resistance had amounted to next to nothing, and in the end those who were against it with all of their souls were simply forced to float away. Oh, there were a few who argued for the jobs that would come, 500 family range employment opportunities, the possibility of business and growth, but they were swallowed up by the fears of the majority. My parents sat in silence while others argued their point: there were children in that neighborhood. Kids. What kind of lives could they look forward to? What kind of environment would spread? How could they do that to children, to good, honest folks who work hard for their money and save and build their own back porches? To the people in the town, it was as if the summer had turned on honesty itself, on everything good and strong, as if something had grown up out of the ground that would spread like disease in a B-grade horror movie.

Lidia

What planted the prison in the town was money. The contractor, the mayor next in line, and the governor had an inviolate relationship. All the righteousness of the town reduced to dirt and hot weather, a spot on the nightly news, until they weren't news anymore, and the news was the finishing touches on the penitentiary and the incoming prisoners, and even past that, until the news was a small town half-emptied and boring and wrinkled like the skin at the knuckles of an old man.

Our house was right at the edge of the thing because we were at the edge of town. My father had been raised in the oil fields near Port Arthur and he'd nearly gone crazy from the black heads bobbing and hemming a body in, the stench, the drive of the drilling animating everything in sight. When he left all he wanted to see was land and sky and nothing else, said it made him feel free, the wide openness, the expanse. My father was mourning something more private of his own making. The distance of geography. The land releasing toward sky. Who knows what my mother thought. I imagined her as a frightened doe. The folds of her brain wrapped themselves around homes for pretty white folks with families, not property for a state penitentiary, not prisoners like a black plague infecting the land.

That great empty expanse that my father loved only made me feel dead. Eyes full of nothing and nothing but endless dirt and rocks and shrubs. In the attic window I'd hunch-sit with a sneaker-glass of tequila and next to nothing on. Everything moved from out of the dark, in the abstract, hazy and wonderful. In a timeless kind of dreamscape I watched red and gray structures emerge from the wasteland of dirt, buildings getting born, architecture reaching in threatening geometry towards the sky. I watched the fencing contain everything, reaching as it did for miles around the place, its silver crisscrossing and walling off this world from that in great sheets of fence. I'd watched ditches being dug and phone lines being unraveled from huge dowels, I'd watched more metal than I thought existed in the universe coming and coming, I'd seen them pour the concrete for all of the sidewalks and paved areas. The sound of construction out there in the heat and dry woke me up in the morning with the light and covered my dreams at night. I dreamed cities emerging, whole populations breeding from within concrete and steel, an urban species clicking and pounding away like a collective machine. The literal meaning of things dissolved. Dreams took up the space of my reality, dreams based on the images pushing up against the little family in the house. Until the prisoners arrived, it was like its own being, artificial, impenetrable, without flesh and yet alive.

If you had asked someone from our town what it was like they would have nothing to say. Partly they were in denial, and so they were in a way thinking the entire event out of existence by ignoring it. Partly they were disaffected because of the humiliating loss, all their efforts leading to defeat. I think that all of the South lives life in this way, its burden pinching up its creative thoughts and twisting them into a life-long defensiveness and blindness.

In fact the day they arrived was a bit anti-climactic. They came in large green buses, they emerged from the vehicles wearing orange suits, single-file, marched from bus to building, disappearing into concrete and wire and metal. Some of the lines of men had handcuffs, some handcuffs and ankle cuffs, some neither. From my window I built a story. This was some kind of hierarchy of crime. I attached meaning and levels of danger to these men; the more dangerous, the more shackles. In reality the men all looked the same, their orange suits smearing them into a single image, their hair and faces repeating endlessly, their footsteps indistinguishable. And the not-knowing a single soul, the anonymity of it nearly made me crazy. Here they were, hundreds of them, soon to occupy tiny rooms and tiny beds in a cage with a toilet and ten steps walking space, and I couldn't feel any...connection. That day I spent drinking and walking ten steps the length of my room, six steps the width of my room, over and over again until I passed out. When I woke it was night, my head swam and hurt. I sat up and took my clothes off, went to

61

my window, looked out into the black speckled with stars.
A breeze carried my imagination over and through, and I
tried to peer in at them one at a time, each sleeping man
in a slightly different position, some tucked in curls like
infants, others straight as boards on their backs, mouths
open. I pictured a man awake like me, trying to see, waiting for something to materialize in front of him, hopeless
but resolved. I could see him. I played a child's game. If I
could see him, he could see me. I touched myself.

Things went on this way for awhile. The penitentiary
just out of reach took up all my thinking. I invented a
hundred sexual fantasies that involved inmates, torture
or escape, violence or the tenderness given after a body
has given up. I moved through fourteen to fifteen almost
dazed, it seemed to me as if nothing at all was happening, as if time was thick and dry like the heat and geography. The people I went to school with had no meaning to
me. Books continued to house me in a way that the world
did not.

The summer of my fifteenth birthday my brother did
not come home. I had a bottle of Jack Daniels, a bottle of
Gilbey's, and tequila under the bed. I spent my days skipping school getting high with guys I barely knew, guys
I'd met through my brother. The more I let them touch
me the more they didn't mind. From my parents I received
used copies of Shakespeare's comedies. I count that summer as one that turned me inside out, a snake shedding
skin, or just the explosion of a body. By that time I was
shooting heroin, but that was not the main thing. By that
time I was making trips from my window to a place 200
yards away from the fence for long hours at a time, waiting in the dark, crouched behind scrub and brush not four
feet high off the ground.

They'd emerge twice a day. Once mid-morning, once
late afternoon. They'd play ball, walk around, cluster in
tight two and three person fists there in the yard. I was
close enough to make out their figures, but not the faces.
Faces blurred into little knobs of heads, and the orange
repetitions made me squint. Binoculars helped, but also

62

made the dull ache harder to bear. My first distant encounters with the fence of their world came at night, alone, dark, wind, nothing. I sat half hidden by bushes two football fields away. Looking at the patterns of fence I could feel the hairs on my arms raising, asking, begging. I'd sit out there and drink, and think, acclimatizing myself to the edge of their world. Then I'd walk home, my feet making crooked, my body not remembering my name, my hands dangling at my sides, fingers itching and twitchy.

All that summer I could hear the electronic drone of the talking heads come up through the vents in the house up to the attic like a televised haunting. Debates and news reports and town halls all revolving around the prison, its inhabitants, its dark center. People wanted proof that the inmates were doing hard time. People didn't want the convicts to have televisions or weight rooms. No luxuries. They're all perverts and degenerates. Doing time is supposed to hurt. How can anyone think of these people as more than animals? I remember thinking, Christ, why do people keep asking that? My thinking is, if you can ask the question, you don't deserve to know the answer. If you haven't read *The Tempest*, don't even talk to me. Someday I'm going to make a bumper sticker that reads: "This thing of darkness I acknowledge mine."

It came to me the day I was skipping an English class, smoking pot with a couple of heads behind the auditorium. Guys that had brothers who knew mine. Guys that had put their hands in my cunt. I was rolling when the idea hit me, the white paper twirling between my fingers, forming itself into itself tight and thin and potent. It was the most simple and clear thing I'd ever done in my life. I asked where they got their shit, they told me a guy's name, told me my brother used to know him, I asked if I could meet him, the action of it took less than a minute. Convincing the guy about my idea was even more simple. Who would suspect someone's sister, girl, little girl bright as light coming to see a man wretched and dismal in his shame? I could already pass successfully enough to buy

63

beer and cigarettes at the 7-11. I could get into the town bar. My brother. He'd fixed me up with an ID—some girl he met at college. Some girl he probably fucked. I swear to god we looked like twins, that unknown girl and me, the faces echoing each other, the two lives touching, burning, alive.

I got the name of the first guy I visited from the guy with the drugs. I passed my ID and the contents of my pockets through a slot at the bottom of a Plexiglas window. I was not wearing any jewelry, nor an underwire bra, nor anything metal, as I'd been instructed by the authorities at the check-in desk. A guard made circles around the edges of my body with a metal detector wand; my skin shivered. My mouth burned. My lips felt too big. I thought I might cry. But that first time my body knew a truth that I did not, my legs carried me as if they had memorized the steps without me.

His name was Earl. His eyes sucked me up into gray-blue pools like I was thin as air. He did not smile, he barely spoke, he put his hand near my collar bone as if he knew me. He was supposed to know me. His hand moved down toward my waist, he squeezed me just under the rib. His face came to me and his image went out of focus as the blurry stubble on his skin got big and he kissed me, not on the mouth but as close as is possible, wet, hot, lingering there before he moved back. I could feel his tongue, spittle. He'd deftly taken a small bag from underneath my shirt in back. My spine shivered, my belly convulsed, my mouth filled with saliva and I had to pee so bad it was painful. I don't know what the story was from the inside. I don't know if I was his niece, or his daughter, or his sister or just some ripe young thing he'd have killed if she tried to run. Nothing formed inside my brain. It was as if my body and my mind had formed a new species. She had emerged. She was coming alive there for the first time in her life.

I saw Earl once a week for about a year.

At night I'd continue my vigils, my hands alive and my body firing its pistons relentlessly. It was as if I had a precise reason to live, as if the world had written itself before me in spite of the dry and barren expanse of my life, and all I had to do was read it into being. Sometimes during visiting hours in the common room I'd give Earl a hand job, or he would me, and we kept on not knowing each other at all, rarely speaking, and the pleasure was so intense I thought I might die. Sometimes a guard would fondle my tits in an empty corridor. Once an inmate came on my hand while Earl and I were getting each other off. And all the time I was reading and reading Shakespeare, and all the words spinning me into my body, and all that I was coming and coming back out and into the very pit of longing, confined behind the walls of the whole world, so it seemed.

65

In my own bed, dreams wrestled me into color and vision, orange to red to blue and back again, armies of men breaking loose from their rooms, breaking walls and heads and bodies, making inside and outside crazy, leaving the stupid human organization of things blown to bits. I saw the logic of the inside out. In books and dreams and inside the penitentiary, between my legs, everything was being reborn. I knew existence through my body and my mind cut as fine as a diamond, pure, without lies. I felt as if no other world existed. No other home, no other skin for the body.

Night wind changes the structure of things. The distance between my room and the prison closed, as if I had forged a dirt river alone over treacherous rocks and reptiles, my little boat body bringing me to the other side, not inside, not outside, and nothing in between, not a woman, nor a girl, nor any hope of an identity, but a chance to reinvent myself endlessly. I became an expert at the logic of waiting, how it housed the forsaken. Like me, the men in that house had the long wait waiting ahead of them, marked off on the wall in chalked scrapes that looked like the marks tires make on pavement when a car screeches away. Like me, the lives of those men were mutating, their bodies turning from one species to another, from hot blooded mammals to the cold belly of something

YUKNAVITCH

Lidia

that had night vision, some animal that could survive in the desert, something from our past about survival and using deprivation as a motivation for life. Like me the life of the vein and an altered state could relieve that mortal coil of ordinariness, the dullness of the way our lives inevitably turn out. Brotherhood.

Whiskey or heroin could keep a girl from letting the dust of a town settle on her, as if these substances kept the molecules moving around at such a pace that even incarceration couldn't hold her, no school, no family, no daughter-life could close around her or bar her vision. I understood the confines and I understood the boundlessness, the way a mind could be forced to bust open and let loose its limits, puny rules and knowledges, little Gods and the fingers of old women. Sometimes I'd bring pills inside my panties. Sometimes pieces of plastic or wood or dope under the cup of each budding, new breast. I was on the right side. I was at the edge of the world; discovery crouched like dreams in my fingertips.

I'd like to say I saw it coming, that I'd so keenly developed a sense of things, so educated myself and poised my own intellect sharp enough to cut. I'd like to say I had expanded my view of the universe, entered realms that only the outcast and extreme individual knows about. But who among us can see a self? Pages and pages have been written. Great minds have failed and failed. On my eighteenth birthday I saw my brother in the yard of the penitentiary, his orange suit brighter than the others, his face in full focus, his hands dangling from his arms like a man's so familiar I couldn't recognize them.

At first I saw him as entering a kind of tribe. I quite quickly wrote the story in my head that he was entering a realm of my own making, a place where reality was not infected with the disease of citizenship and socially condoned organization. I felt a kind of pride. I even felt as if I had readied the environment in some small way for him, that I had given years of my life to the beat of its heart, the blood running through its veins. That I was privy to the inner-workings of the underbelly of society, and that

66

we would find a deeper relationship there than blood could ever afford.

The first time he saw me, during a visitation period with Earl in the common room, he ignored me completely. He looked straight through me. His eyes were blue-gray stones, as if he didn't know me from Adam.

I signed up to see him immediately.

The glass between us, black phones in our hands, our eyes locked on faces from a family, mouths on the edge of speaking.

"Hello."

Silence.

I was hot and excited. My breathing seemed to be jack-knifing in my lungs. My words flew out in all directions, uncontainable. "What are you in for? You shocked my shit, the day I saw you. Do the folks know? I don't think they do. No one has said anything at dinner…so, what are you in for?" My little voice technologically reduced between us.

Silence.

His eyes crept up my collar bone and rested some-where between my jaw and my chin. I babbled on, "It doesn't matter. How long are you—"

"Shut up. Listen to me. I'm only going to say this once. I want you to hang up. I want you to hang up, stand up, turn around, walk out of here, and never fucking come back."

"Don't be ridiculous. You think you are the only rea-son I'm here? I've been here hundreds of times. It's no big deal. I just thought I'd…"

"Shut up. Shut the fuck up." He raised his hand and made a kind of fist that reflected in the glare of the glass. The two fists hovered there like question marks, threat-ening. "I know why you are here. I've fucking heard all about it."

"What are you talking about?"

"You're famous. You're the talk of the town here."

"I don't have a goddamn idea in hell what you are talking about. People here know me. They are used to me, is all. I know the name of—"

"You don't get it, do you. You stupid fucking bitch. You ignorant infant. You want to know what they call you around here? Do you? They call you Hole. Just Hole. You're like this child that spreads her legs and humps any guy who wants it. There's pictures of you—little cartoons all over this fucking place. There's little poems about you, about your pussy, the way you put out, about how you are a little whore and how you'd suck the dick of a dead man."

"You're lying. You're a fucking liar. I know the scene here a lot better than you. Back off. Don't try to fucking dick with me. Look. If somebody said those things it's a lie. People here know me. Guards. Inmates. They're used to me. They work with me. Give me shit. I sell it. Or I get shit for them. Like you used to do."

"Yeah? Well how come I can get a play-by-play description of what you do and a detailed description of your pussy from any guy in here?"

"You're lying. You just want me to go."

"You know that guy you been fucking? Well he has a big-ass mouth."

"Shut up. He's not like that at all. We have an understanding. Look, stop being such a prick. I haven't seen you in years. I just wanted to see you. Tell me how long you are in for."

"You stupid cunt. You gullible dumb cunt. You must have shit for brains."

"Fuck you! You don't know me at all. I've got my own life, my own money. I've worked hard for it. I thought you'd be glad to see me. I'm all you've got. I'm leaving soon—when I'm gone no one will know you are here. Don't you want to talk?"

"You're an ignorant hole. You know what happens to me when they find out in here that I'm related to your stank pussy? I get butt-fucked, for starters. I'm marked for life. I'm fucking marked. Do you get it, miss fucking little dick dancer? You may as well shove a joy stick up me right now. I'll be a toy, I'll be the toast of the town. And while you're getting your fucking fancy ass degree,

68

which you can shove up your cunt like everything else, I'll be a dead man in here."

"That's a crock of shit. What are you talking about? Nobody cares about me. I'm nothing to them. I just sell drugs, supply, like you did."

"Goddamn, you really don't know shit, do you. Don't you know there is a hierarchy in here? You think I'm in here for selling some puny-ass lid? Look again. I'm here for fucking little girls, sister. Pedophiles are on the bottom of the heap, baby, and I've got a little underage whore for a sister to boot. Don't you get it? I'm fucked. *Fucked, little sister, and I didn't even get a piece of your ass. I should have fucked you when I had the chance.*"

Did I lose my mind? Had he?

I tore loose from his ugly mouth and the echo of those words like some scared animal. I ran. I ran from that room and his hand on that black phone and his voice coming through that glass and his face. I ran down the linoleum hall and past the fondling guards, smirking, laughing, touching themselves, I ran past the check-in desk and out the colossal metal doors, doors I'd watched being built and located, I ran down the concrete path, concrete I'd seen poured, past some men in the yard, their orange suits laughing like mouths, clicking like sparks, I ran against chain link and sky, I ran to the gate and it was closed and I climbed it, I clawed my way up, guards with guns drawn pulling at my heels and tears and spit and my head pounding like crazy. I growled and kicked all the way down, and they were laughing, they saw who I was and they started laughing, and when they got me to the ground, pinned and wriggling there on the asphalt, saying hold on now, hold on, we're just trying to help you dammit, calm down now, holding my wrists and thighs, I was screaming, I was taking all the voice in me and screaming out to that big sky, to the men holding me down, to all the men in that place that I had given myself to, to the walls, the fences, the whole architecture, I was screaming, he loved me, he did, forty thousand brothers could not with all their quantity of love make up the sum, and an ambulance came, and men standing in the yard would say later that crazy bitch finally lost it, and didn't she have a sweet pussy, all pink and sticky like the open mouth of a child, didn't she just?

70

The Garden of Earthly Delights

Bosch centers his vision on the forehead of the clock and says *seven, eight, nine.* He's been on this shift for nine months. On at six, off at twelve, on again at six, off again on again. Salmon and sea bass slide beneath hands, his hands palming and fingering the scales and the touch of slime, his breath sucking in the sea and the guts of thousands and thousands of slit-open bellies.

Pimply boy next to him, bleached blonde hair, fingers like an artist; *he won't last a month, or else he will, he'll be reborn and vex his family.* His thoughts curl around the boy like water. Bosch already wants to take the pimply boy home. He can't help it. In the small and gray-green of things the boy sticks out like delight. He can smell his hair. His mind's eye is visioning the boy's head resting on his chest, he's thinking of showing him the ropes, how to take care of his hands, how to sleep awake, how to turn the body to cruise control and let the limbs, hands, move themselves, thoughtless. Something about his face. How young in the eyes. How little membranes stretch over the blueness, like the film of a fish eye lensing-over sight.

The boy is smoking in the alley after the shift, his left foot up against the side of the building, the cigarette drooping from his lip and his hands shoved down so hard in his pockets he looks armless. What else to think of an image like that except this is what a boy looks like, hunched and smoking in the night, his whole life ahead of him but his body resisting itself. Wanting but not. It is too easy to offer him scotch from an inside pocket all warm and surrender. It is easier yet to take him home after maybe ten minutes of not saying anything, just passing the bottle back and forth, just their breath hanging suspended in the white cold night air there before them. Home to a one room house packed to wood walls with one small black stove, one square white ice-box, one makeshift bed, one toilet behind a curtain, one window, asking night.

72

"Nice place," know-nothing says.

"Works for me."

"Bet you never expected this, huh?"

"What?" Bosch begins the slow undoing of layers of clothing, his skin hot and cold at the same time.

"*This.*" The boy's clothes shed themselves, his collarbone and shoulders dipping and curving, his hands hanging down the length of his arms.

Bosch thinks and thinks what *this* means, is it the boy before him, his crotch bulging up like prayer between them, the gap of not knowing each other at all luscious and ripe and making him salivate? How long the wait, or was *this* his whole life, the long wait waiting again and again until new seasons and tides and moons turned the world over? The boy's lips puff out; *mamma's boy*, Bosch thinks, only it's nothing but a mouthful of bliss.

The room heats up in nothing flat, stars illuminate their naked. Bosch can't see his own hands, but his hands find the form, working and reaching and sliding their way along. The boy is no longer a boy, he is swimming beneath Bosch, he is licking and teasing, he is moving in the underwater of night. Breathing forgets itself back to its blue past. Their mouths gape and suck.

Two faces pointing up toward the surface of the night. He tells him about the last boy his age to come through. People saw him out there in the nothingness making a goddamn snowman with his bare hands, frostbite, but the dumb motherfucker didn't know it, pumped himself up so full of acid he had two numb clubs for hands, came to work, worked the row without the massive yellow rubber gloves, until someone finally looked over and said *Jesus God—look at that, he's got meat for hands.* And they took him away with those red and useless weights of flesh hanging from the ends of his arms, and he lost one of them; boy couldn't have been more than twenty-two years old.

"That's the trouble...you're all fucked up on dope and shit half the time. A guy could get himself into a lot of shit out here that way. There's no room for error. You have to find the rhythm of the place, being here. It's a whole different existence. Don't come to work fucked up. I'm telling you right now. Guys'll take advantage of you, try to mess you up, because if you are out then their pay goes up. All you young guys come out here, college boys, trying to score the big bucks over the summer so you can quit waiting tables during the year, or buy some shitty-ass car, or more dope, or whatever it is you do. Just...all I'm saying is, watch yourself. Pay attention. Get into the rhythm of it. You'll be all right."

The boy runs his fingers over Bosch's stomach, light as feathers, flesh whispers. Everything inside of him, intestines, muscles, squirms and lifts in the direction of touch.

He is in the bed of his childhood, in his mother's house. His father has been gone for two years now. His father a no-good his father a cook at a diner his father a clerk at a 7-11 his mother needing to feed her baby. It is night. The front door is rattling and cracking and splitting open with his mother and a man. Laughter brings the bodies into the house; he holds his breath, his heart dull thudding in his ears. He is sweating under covers from not moving. Not breathing. They career off edges, furniture, cacophonous, they nearly crash through the wall of his room; no. They are going to her room, to his parent's room, blue walls, blue bed, perfume and a mirror.

In the morning a man driving away in a Pinto wagon. Bosch eating cereal, his hair arguing with itself, his hands little fists around spoon and bowl. He stares at the milk, the flakes floating there, bobbing up and down, he stares and stares at anything but the tired woman entering the kitchen smelling old and distilled and too sweet. Something—breathing? Something gives him away.

"What are you looking at you little shit? You ain't gonna find any answers in your Wheaties, that's for goddamn sure!" Snorts of laughter. "Hey. I'm talking to you. Hey Mr. Man of the house. When are you going to get a fucking job and start earning your keep? I can't keep stuffing your little fat face with food, you know. You're old enough to take care of yourself. Goddamn little sucker-fish, that's what you are, a bottom-dweller. Suck suck suck. You make me sick."

Bosch looks up for a slow second before she leaves the room with a bottle of Jack Daniels. He sees her eyes magnified and blurry, he sees bubbles escaping from her mouth instead of words, his mind drifts away from her without sound, water filling his ears, his nose, his mouth. Only his heart beats out a rhythm. She is dissolving from sight, she is nearly invisible, wait, she has disappeared in a wave of stained silk.

The boy's name is Aram, and he is out of vision, down and down the line from Bosch. Now and again he can see a patch of bleached blonde out of the corner of his eye, and he is glad. His own flesh seems warmer than before, warm-blooded, he can feel his own pulse and his hands glide and cup and dive between fish bodies as never before. His neck does not ache in a knot at the base of his head after three hours, his vertebrae do not feel leaded and distorted when he has an hour left, his feet do not throb and spike with the day coming down on them. It is as if his mind is coming back to him in small increments.

He sees an image of Aram gently turning in the night, his torso white and the muscles of his back barely emerged, the fin of his rib guiding his sleep. The odor of blood and waste mingles with his image of the boy, and the image overtakes the present moment, he breaths in the sight, he lets go the work, his body moves without thought, his mind's eye deep in the dark memory, or is it the future, coming to him like a pool of water?

Aram puts his mouth over Bosch's cock. He can see the woodstove and its little light just behind the boy's head appearing and then not, like that, in the dark of night. His own member sucks thought from his brain, as if the body could will the mind into instinct and primal drive. He closes his eyes and when he cums it is into the mouth of the world, young and in the shape of an "O." He is lost there. A boy's mouth takes him out of himself. He places his hands on Aram's head, he can see the brightness of his hair, halo-like and for a moment, stunning. He is caught there for a moment, dazed and electrified all in the same moment.

In Seattle there were jobs, but the boys emerging from Issaquah and Chehalis and Sequim were malformed somehow, their bodies too white, or twisted away from offices and college degrees. A high school diploma was simply a ticker tape running across his forehead for anyone to see, saying *I do not speak your language, you must speak more slowly, what are the directions, where are we going?* They had a different smell and habitat, even their hair and shoulders looked different. Contained and quick smart like the click of heels on pavement. When he'd landed a job at the corner bar as a bus boy his mother had said, "That fucking figures. You're just like your father, aren't you, pretty boy? I just hope you can do something for a lady with those hands, that's all he had going for him, I can tell you, mister. You sure got shorted on the brains, and come to think of it, the brawn too. Ain't nothing in this life gonna come easy to you. You got big lips like a mamma's boy, too. I bet you get your nose busted before you're eighteen." And she laughed with the open mouth of a bass, huge and obscene and devouring.

Nights he'd come home and she wouldn't be there, and then she would, him in his room of a world with earphones closed so tight around his skull his lips puckered, music pounding so hard it outdid his heart. She'd bang on the door or even open it, swagger there, framed by the disconnected air around them, foreign and malevolent but without origins. Then she'd cry, or shout obscenities at him.

Other nights men would come, men with hair greased black slick as a record album and with teeth missing, or with the leathery skin of alcohol and marbled eyes swimming in their little sockets. Once he saw her walking naked to the bathroom in the earliest hours of morning. Her breasts dropped down like dangling glass globes. Her face appeared to wear a map of things. Her shoulders sank, as if her spine had given over years ago, her ass dipped in instead of out, and her belly, rotund and hard as a melon, balled out from her spine, almost as a child's. She'd fallen to the floor just in front of the bathroom that morning, and in the bruised light and half-consciousness of the vision he'd watched her wriggle there on the floor before turning her head back, contorted and begging, in the direction of his room, her mouth slit downward in a terrible arc. He simply closed his door, not listening, not thinking, not being anything at all. In his bed his mind made waves, *I am weightless, I am as if adrift and nothing.*

The boy lasts, Aram takes time from one month to two and to three, from three to four, and in the space of half of a year the young man and Bosch swim through labor into deep undulations of form and heat. Fatigue takes on new definitions as their desire wets itself. Physical pain multiplies and deforms into ecstasy like hours on a clock, endlessly repeating, until there is no telling night from day, pleasure from torture, a single room from the cavities of the body.

Hot coffee between palms; dusk.

"Did you think it would be like this?"

"No. Yes. I mean the work. Yes."

"And this?"

"You?"

"Me?"

Who is speaking, Bosch thinks, and who are we that we lose ourselves?

Bosch neither nods nor signals his hands nor reflects any answer in his eyes. He just sits there looking at the beautiful boy in his one room world, the blonde fire-headed boy who gives light to a dark making.

"No. I didn't figure there would be anyone like you out here. And I wasn't thinking about anything…well, happening." Aram slides from his chair over the edge of the bed where Bosch is sitting like an old beast of some sort. Hunched over and quizzical in the face. He entwines himself—arms, legs, torso—in between the lines of Bosch's body, in between the spaces where flesh meets flesh, where limbs move away like fins, everywhere of him. He makes soft cooing noises.

Bosch closes his eyes and tries to remember this feeling for when it is gone. For it will be gone, will it not, that is the way of things, that is time, and time is a fucker, and except for this one time in all of his life he didn't care about the boot-sludge drone of time at all, and suddenly it is everything, isn't it, it is the whole of life and death stuffed into a tiny room with not enough oxygen to breath or keep a fire going. It is strange to be remembering before the thing itself is gone from you, strange to have that pressure; memorize, fold the images and the impressions of skin into gray labyrinth of the brain. Picture them over and over again in the mind's eye, day and night, like repeating words endlessly, like the never-ending glow of white on white.

"I don't want to know you, I just want to know the idea of you," Bosch says, almost begging.

"But we do know each other," he grins, he is too blonde, "we keep knowing each other more and more."

And he traces lines on Bosch's back, up and over the
shoulder to his chest and heart, as if he knows the way,
knows it by heart, every vein, every scar, every road of
skin or thought since before he was born. Bosch's heart
beats too heavy in the chest, it tightens and squeezes into
a hard ball. His face twists as if he might cry, then releases
itself. What is a boy what is a boy what is a boy.

He has a black eye, a shiner from a man he's never
met except in the hallway of his mother's home. A black
eye as black as the night he got it, and for no reason that
he could tell, just there at the wrong time, wrong place,
wrong world, sledgehammer hand big man drunk coming down the hall at him saying "What the fuck are you
grinning at? I'm gonna slap that goddamn grin right off
your face." Alone in his room with his stinging face
pressed against the wood grain of the door he hears them
arguing, the rise and fall of voices, the rise and fall of fists
or the sound of something breaking, a lamp, a glass, a rib.
She is all mouth, his mother, she can rage on with the best
of them, she doesn't flinch, she's gutsy that way. But then
he hears her incomprehensibly quiet. His whole head
against the door he hears her not at all. He hears the lumbering dull and swollen thick man banging his way out
of the house, wall to wall to floor and up and out, slamming out, wheels peeling out, Camaro screeching away.
Nothing nothing nothing from the other side.

Sweat forms on his upper lip and it is cold. His face is
swollen and wet and white. His knuckles, white. He bangs
his head gently against the door once.

"Mother."

Nothing.

He opens the door to his room and crosses the stream
of the hallway to her room. He opens her door. There she
is as he pictured she would be, stretched out on the floor
in a kind of "s" shape, her mouth bloody, her eyes puffy,
her peach satin negligee twisted up her torso, the blue of
the shag carpet floating her still body.

"Mother."

78

He helps her up, helps her to the bed. She is not dead. Just submerged and bleary-eyed. She is mumbling and slurring and her mouth slides around. "I've got to get it out of here," she is saying and saying. He tells her he's gone now, I'll lock and bolt the door. He's gone. He puts ice in a dish towel and soap on another. He washes her face and holds the cold to her eyes and mouth. Her lips bulge and the words keep spilling out, she shakes her head no and no. "Out of me, it's in there." He thinks, what is it like for a woman to get fucked like that. It is foreign to him. Like another species. He cannot imagine. Nothing about her seems like him.

After she swims towards sleep in her slurry speech he goes back to his room. Just before dawn he thinks of ice-caps and the white expanse of Alaska. He thinks of an ocean bearing us away into an Arctic otherworld.

He takes off his hood, unzips his gigantic red parka. The down shape of him shrinks, like he is removing layers of himself, like a Russian doll within a doll within a doll. He pulls his wool sweater over his head by reaching at it from the back. His hair ruffles. He unbuttons the silver tabs on his Levi's. Not one at a time but in a swift pull from the top, so that they all pop in a single motion. He then stretches his torso down and up to take off his T-shirt; his nipples harden instantaneously. His lip quivers for a moment. He inches his long-johns down goose-pimpled legs, over muscle and knee and bone to ankle, twists each foot out. Down his boxers. He is a naked boy. He is beautiful and almost absolutely still. His breathing is the only thing that moves. Bosch feels as if he might weep. Bosch can smell the sex of him. Sweet sweat and soap and skin. His cock grows, pulses up red between them. Bosch's mouth is watering and his hands ache at the ends of his leaded arms.

He wants to hold him like an infant, he wants him to suck at his tit while he rocks him and squeezes his cock. He pictures an almost perfect medieval painting of Madonna and child. He nearly vomits from desire before he reaches out to touch him.

79

They wrestle-fuck on the floor. As Bosch is driving into him he is also handling the boy's cock in front. The boy is arching hard back so that his head is in the place between Bosch's shoulder and neck; he can see the boy's face, contorted angel. The boy cums first all over himself and all over Bosch's hand and Bosch can see the milk-white spray and his own release pulses out of him up and inside. The boy says he can feel it in his spine and lets out a kind of laugh, glorious. The boy says, "I want to stay like this forever, I never want anything to change, it's this that I waited for my whole life, this feeling." Bosch thinks sentences give us hope in all the wrong ways, language tortures us into faith. What's true is that they can only stay like that on the floor until the heat begins to die in the room. Eventually Bosch has to get dressed, go out to the wood shed, and refill the woodstove. He leaves the boy thinking, he'll get into the bed, and then we can sleep for a few hours. He leaves the boy but keeps the smell of him sucked nearly all the way to his heart as he enters the outside white.

When he awakens Bosch hears birds. He thinks of a boat taking him to Alaska, of seagulls. But then it is not birds. It is fainter. It is human. He comes conscious and understands it is the little whimper of a boy; no. It is his mother whimpering. He goes to her room. She is not there. He goes to the sound. She is in the bathroom. It is barely light. Something smells wrong. He does not want to open the door, and then he does, and there they are on the white floor, mother and child, a little red and blue lump of fetus curled near her. Five months, six? His mother is so pale she looks dead. As if she ran out of oxygen hours ago. Her mouth opens and closes. Her hand twitches for an instant. He bends down and looks at things. It is a boy. It was.

At the woodshed it is clear that more wood needs splitting. Bosch considers not taking the time, then remembers how much the boy likes to sleep, how his sleep swells the room with the smell of a world starting over. He decides that an hour will have no meaning to a beautiful, sleeping boy. Let the boy dream. Let sleep take him away and underneath the surface of things. Let the image of death be reborn in a boy, every single night. With each heave he lets loose a terrible and mindless sobbing. He fills his arms with wood; there is no weight heavy enough to release him.

Later, maybe two hours later, with arms full of wood he has trouble opening the door, but then it gives, and a great whoosh of warm air hits the incoming cold. It's a wonder lightning doesn't form from their meeting like that, man and boy, or some electrical charge, some white spark cracking between inside and outside. There he is, unmoved on the floor where he left him, a beautiful pale smile on his face, his eyes closed, lashes painted down onto cheeks. His arms are stretched out on either side, his blue veins making rivers across his infant-thin skin at the wrists. *There is no other heaven than this,* Bosch thinks, *this is heaven on earth,* and he closes the door and builds the fire like a new faith for all of the white against them.

81

Against Interpretation

I remember the first time I got it. That Sontag thing.
During this time I was screwing a deconstructionist.
Well, two. One was a wanna-be, the other the thing itself. The thing about a deconstructionist is they won't
hold still. Am I right? Slippery little suckers, aren't they?
Always fading from focus, too. You know what I mean.
It's like playing hide and seek with Nietzsche. God is
dead. Olly-olly-umcomphree. Go fish. Good looking
sons-of-bitches though. Anyway. We all three met inside this Sontag text. Inscribed by her ideas. They both
had opinions, needless to say, about how important her
ideas had been *at the time*. And I remember thinking, in
both cases, gee, brainiacs, what *time* was that? Do you
mean the 1960s? I thought deconstructionists understood time out of history, history as discourse, chro-
nology as flap-jawed nonsense. *At the time*. Well hell.
Like our man Bill Shakespeare was important *at the time*.
Of course I know what they meant. I'm just saying it
was hypocritical. Get my meaning? But I didn't really
have anything to prove, so I just let it go at that. I wanted
to fuck, not fight.

I don't know why the hell I went to grad school. I don't know why I chased down a PhD. I know I wasn't like anyone else who was there, and I know that I don't have, or I have not achieved the things I was supposed to. But neither did I get spit out, booted, 86'd. Curious. At any rate, I was there, I was waving Marx and Hegel around like a flag of my disposition, I was shamelessly throwing names like Jameson and Deleuze and Guattari and Bakhtin around with the best of them. My lips were fluttering away, bubbles emerged from my mouth as with all the others. I wore black. I wore stylish Brooks Brothers glasses. I had silver jewelry. I talked the talk. I said Julia Kristeva. Georg Lukács. I said Walter Benjamin. Whole lexicons uttered like secret decoder ring child's games. And when I was horny, I very methodically and with potent research skills set out to get what I wanted. Isn't that what intelligence is in a woman? Don't give me that crap about equality and mental chessmanship. I didn't want to be smarter than any of the men I knew. I wanted to be as smart as they were and fuck the brains out of every goddamn last one of them. So let's be frank. Screwing outweighed education by a billion years. To hell with that deferral shit. You know what's what.

So you can understand how it was that when I read about an erotics of art I thought I was way ahead of the fucking game. Because I understood the hermeneutic implications of pretty much everything I read also happened at the level of an ordinary body, and I'd sit there in my apartment bathroom naked, perhaps taking a dump, and think, yeah, so? It's not as if anything in all of pukey human history has ever changed because some painfully brilliant person wrote down their ideas. We keep killing and fucking and eating each other no matter what; it only shifts forms, not content. That's something I could never figure out about my so-called *colleagues*. I mean, they actually thought they were traveling, I mean in the literal sense, via ideas. Wherewherewhere did they get to? Where has the world gotten to? The best response appears to me to be scotch and fucking. Eternally.

But I digress. About fucking. Not much to say, is there? I mean, it is not as if I have anything new to add to the great saga of academic boinking. Or in particular, the academia variety—male professor and young woman student, female professor and young male student, cross-lateral gay and lesbian advances, student-to-student escapades, yawn. Crossword puzzles. And God knows in 1999 we all have a pretty solid script of the power structure of fucking—presidents and interns, teachers and students, priests and altar boys, day-care center leaders and children, fathers and daughters, I mean, Foucault is old news at this point. Smart boy, stylish guy, but old news. Am I right?

So the one guy, the wanna-be, he had a red-headed girlfriend to beat all. She had big tits and huge flowing red hair and the greatest mouth that ever threw lips over a cock. I mean really, I don't think any men appreciated her as much as I did. She was a fucking knockout in the 50s Hollywood sense, and she wore clothing from that era as well. Jesus. I'm telling you. Her eyes were bright blue, too, and her name was Erica. Can you picture this? I believe that you can.

Anyway, the deconstructionist wanna-be used to have my boyfriend and I over for dinner parties and so forth. They lived in the woods in this great old house that had been left to Erica by her grandparents. Midsummer night's dream is the phrase that comes to mind when I think of going out to Erica's house. She had this great Japanese goldfish pond, and a string of Chinese paper lanterns leading off into the woods. There was a spare building with a loft sleeping area that she used as a sculpture studio, and get this, she always worked naked. No shit. The kitchen had dried herbs and roses hanging upside down all over the place, and she had her own mini-vineyard out back—made her own wine. Fantastic hooch. Knocked you on your ass in twenty minutes. Get the picture?

So we're out there one night and we're drunk and stoned and everything is dreamy and swelling with great deep reds and oranges and the smell of gardenia. Or something. And at a certain point late in the evening, four of us, me and mine, Erica and the wanna-be deconstructionist, begin to shed our clothing and fondle one another in a group. The rest of the people at the dinner party settle in on couches and huge pillows scattered about the floor for optimum viewing. This is after we had pierced Rachel's navel with a safety pin and all the women had kissed one another in passionate lip locks for the hell of it. After my boyfriend and the wanna-be deconstructionist had sucked one another's cocks on a dare, after the fat guy from Fresno had taken a dive into the goldfish pond, after the shy girl with no eyebrows had disappeared and re-emerged dressed in an eighteenth century corset from Erica's eccentric wardrobe. OK?

So the wanna-be is going down on me (don't ask me
how he got my pants off—I'd rigged them closed with all kinds of pins and shit because I'd just bought them at a vintage clothing store and didn't have time to sew them into normalcy), and Erica, as I turned my head to the side in a kind of giddy sleeplessness, is riding my boyfriend for all he's worth. The only problem is, he's a bit flaccid, as happens with too much to drink and too many drugs, so actually she's just riding to be riding, and she is the most goddamn beautiful image I've ever seen, she's uncanny, she's Napoleon riding in his revolutionary way, she's conquering nations, she's the turn of the century, she's taking no prisoners, she's trampling the dead. Somewhere in that watching I come, the wanna-be's mouth fills with it, he moans and gurgles, I remember there is a man between my legs and let go the superb aesthetics of her image.

So I look at his face down there, sort of perched on my cunt and between the mountains of my thighs and knees. His eyebrows are working furiously, more furiously than when he is being a deconstructionist wanna-be and going on and on about the use and abuse of history and catachresis and on and on, and suddenly his eyes lurch up to my face (his head stays put, mind you), and we clap eyes on one another, we are locked there in that duel, his mouth to my mouth, he thinks he is making me come, I am an observer entirely, my cunt is the object of my performance, distanced, sadistic, pure. I am without a self, I am a free-floating sub-jectivity, an as-yet unfinished sentence, the whole she-bang.

Then we're just naked smelly animals again, a little confused, trying to get our clothes back on as the watch-ers try to decide whether they are disgusted or titillated.

The second guy is more of a cliché thing. We're in his office at the university, which of course could be any uni-versity. He turns the lights off. His books and books lin-ing the walls are like ghosts of entire epochs crowding the room. An audience. His Gap button-down shirt is like Siberia. Perfect white on white. His black pants draw me in as a ravine. I can barely see his face, barely see his lips moving. He says, there are things we can do without it meaning we're having sex. His cologne is so much louder than what he is saying, not to mention the fact that what he is saying is so goddamn ludicrous it is beyond belief, and anyway, all women know, even twenty-five-year-old women know what desire is, what cunts and cocks are, what power is, he is so deluded it becomes part of the reason he is irresistible to me, I feel as if I might devour him. And he unbuttons my pants and sticks his living hand (Keats scholar—I can't be with him without the lines invading my head) into that wet salty cunty place and I undo his Geoffrey Beene belt and unzip his Calvin Klein pants and grab his cock hard and to the flesh and so there we are in that office with our hands full like hundreds of other idiots exactly like us with their hands full.

I don't know why things like this come to me at times like that. I said, and no I'm not kidding, and no I haven't an idea in hell why anyone ever behaves as if they don't see the centrifugal force of desire when it's as obvious as it is, big as a fat red clown nose, I said, I want to come on your book, and no I don't know why he reached for his recently published from Stanford beautiful purple cov-ered book and helped me to negotiate a better position for coming, and yes I did.

And that's what I'm saying. About art and desire.

ECONOMIC ICONOGRAPHY

Blood Opus

1. for god and country

Technology? You're asking me about technology? A sick joke. After two years with my unit, never having shot anyone face to face, I was arrested. You know why? Because of my car. The car had been traced to my organization. No one gave me away. They had next to no information on me, which means that no one gave them any. Not that I was important in the organization; I wasn't. I wasn't doing anything of importance that day. I don't even remember what I was doing that day at all. A policeman asked me for my ID, and then he told me to get out of the car. I remember getting out of the car and keeping my eyes on the car, on the door of the car, on the place where the door of the car is connected to the body of the car, the metal, the grease, the car part fashioned in such a way as to let a hunk of metal swing open and closed, open and closed. The policeman had my arm and I was looking at the capability of a car door to swing open or closed.

I was taken to a police station. There was a table in the second room. A man and a woman tied me to the table. Like this: my back was hanging over the edge. When I would try to lift myself up they would hit me. Mostly the woman hit me. I stopped trying to lift myself up only as a choice between two things, up or down.

Then they brought in a vat of water. They shoved my head into it. Then they would lift my head out of the vat by my hair, and back in, and so on. At first I just held my breath and tried to keep my heart rate down. Of course they began to hold my head down long enough and lift it out for a short enough amount of time that soon I was gasping and panting like an animal. It was not frightening. It seemed ridiculous; a head bobbing up and down like that, a face gasping and sputtering, a woman dunking a skull into a tub like a child's party game.

90

2. child's play

Throwing stones was a girl child's play and first duty. When you threw one you knew you were doing something. If you could be imprisoned for studying, why not fight? It is easy to not scream as a child. I witnessed a girl being dragged by a soldier. By her hair. And hitting her on the ground. With his boot. She did not scream. Then she got up and ran. He followed her onto a roof. Beating her again, and telling her he would throw her over. You know what she said? She told him to go on then. He was so baffled he let her go.

Another story.

A girl's throwing stones when she sees a soldier taking aim at a boy. She throws her coat over the boy and pulls him away. Then the soldier aims and shoots at her. She runs to a bus, but the soldier is following her so she runs out the back of a store and onto a balcony. She jumps off, onto a roof, and escapes.

3. forefathers

7. EXT. A BATTLEFIELD

Scarred dirt clumps paths interrupted by stinging black barbed wire here and there. Fog. The smell of mud and decaying flesh (this can be achieved by using meat from the butcher's and fans, along with real mud and dirt, to create an earthy/fleshy stench). Scrap metal, defunct rifle parts, supplies, almost a table, almost a tent, the memory of trench warfare.

ARTILLERY OFFICER: Well I'll be damned. The good preacher is coming from his infantry post to visit.

CHAPLAIN: God be with you, you brave fellows. God bless your weapons. Are you pounding away the enemy?

OFFICER: It's going very well—in the sky—you can hear the raging, the glory. You can see the firing and killing like a show of lights. Why, it's like Christmas. Especially at night. Beautiful.

CHAPLAIN: With God's grace, I'd like to try a gun for once.

(Chuckling from the one or two men around.)

OFFICER: Let's hope you hit one.

(Chaplain fires. Into the empty air. Cheers of Bravo.)

OFFICER: Now that the chaplain has fired, our weapons are blessed.

(Woman reporter approaches.)

HANNAH: What sort of position is this? Is this supposed to be a position? I've seen better positions before. You know what? I'd like to shoot a little bit.

OFFICER: I'd be glad to let you, madam, but unfortunately, it's impossible right now, it could rouse the enemy.

HANNAH: Don't be ridiculous. No one is fighting on the ground. No one has for a hundred years. I just want to shoot it. You let him, but you won't let me? When I've come all this way just for that reason? As you know, I report only from personal experience—keep in mind that I absolutely must finish my story—it's for the upcoming edition! Give it to me. Okay, how is it fired?

OFFICER: Like this—

(Hannah fires. The enemy answers fire.)

OFFICER: See what's happened!

HANNAH: Well I'll be goddamned.

(Everyone stares into the empty fog, the distance, the uninhabited ground under war.)

OFFICER: My God.

HANNAH: Jesus Christ. What do you want? At least it's been interesting, hasn't it? Look. The lights.

(Scene Change.)

91

YUKNAVITCH

Lidia

4. cunt

They did it over and over for three days. On the fourth day they brought me into a different, smaller room. There was a phone on a table. They forced me to telephone my house and tell my friends and family that I was staying with someone, so that no one would think that I had disappeared. That was frightening, because after I hung up the phone I knew that no one would think anything was wrong. They kept telling me they could make me disappear, and I could see that what they were telling me had a certain truth to it.

A phrase I heard from America keeps running like a ticker tape across my forehead at the most ridiculous moments: war on crime.

Then they put a plastic bag over my head. Have you ever tried to breath with a plastic bag over your head? Of course you haven't. They said many things about my family, about my mother and father, about my children, and how they would find them and torture them. That was also frightening, to imagine my children burning, to picture my mother and father humiliated to death. The things they said and did were believable.

Then they began to talk of raping me, because they tell all women this, because they can. A man did not do it to me. A woman did it with a truncheon. I don't know. How does one answer that? I don't know. Not like anything I had ever felt. I could hear her grunting. She was saying obscenities to me too, about being a mother, dirty, deviant in the most hideous of ways.

I broke because I had to break. There is no question on this issue.

5. birthmarks

One of the most maneuverable ever built. Capable of withstanding nine times the force of gravity in steep turns with internal fuel tanks loaded. Loss of consciousness of the pilot sometimes occurs. Mach 2 with a combat ceiling higher than 50,000 feet and a combat range of 340 miles. Equipped with an M-61A1 20mm cannon and 500 rounds of ammunition, it has a 32-foot-8-inch wingspan and measures 49 feet 5 inches long. It weighs up to 42,300 pounds and is powered by a single turbofan engine generating up to 27,600 pounds of thrust.

6. *crimes against humanity*

Main Targets: Politicians, police, the Civil Guard; Some new action in moral and ecological fields, including industries threatening the environment, cinemas and businesses selling products that exploit women, drug dealers.

Main Actions: Bombing, shootings, kneecapping (especially concerning drug dealers).

Media: Monthly communiqués, Self-published newspaper.

Recent attacks: Car, ammunitions, and advanced technology factories, attempted assassination of high ranking gov. officials, murder of two policemen and soldiers, bombing of offices of construction companies, advanced technology factories, letter bombs to Public Works department and other federally funded organizations and buildings.

Note: Frequently issues statements of apology for the killing of non-targeted civilians or workers, terming the violence "accidental injuries involuntarily caused." In one such statement, issued shortly after the flurry of letter bombs opened by postal employees in 1990, the advice was also given to "keep unreferenced individuals from opening mail that is not addressed to them." The organization frequently issues statements about their desires to avoid what they term "painful outcomes."

7. *law enforcement*

The "coffin" is a cell, 1.7 meters high by 80 by 60 centimeters. The walls are made of concrete and the door of iron panels. Prisoners detained in the coffin are not allowed to use the toilet so they urinate, defecate, and vomit all over themselves. We do not baby our prisoners. Criminals are not human, after all.

8. *bearing witness*

I do not know how to write about this. No one will understand. If I use the word "happy," for instance. Think of it. For instance. She told me her arrival at the training camp was the beginning of the happiest period in her life. She told me the camp was in the mountains and the training was hard. Outside. It was very cold, even in summer, and they lived in tents spread over the mountainside. She told me that she did not notice the hardships because she was so happy—happy that at last her dream to become a fighter had come true. Now, finally, she was doing something to stop the occupation of her country. She told me that she was so happy that for the first three days and nights she could not sleep.

9. *women and children first*

Her hands: smally curious. A machine that converts energy into mechanical motion sits still before her on the floor. She began with electric, then spring driven, then hydraulic—she's fascinated by propulsion—but this one's dead without consumption of a fuel. Once her mother told her how to make a battery using a potato. She laughs to herself at the logic of this. She runs her fingers like gentle fish over and under either rods and pistons or something else unimaginable. She has taken it apart piece by piece. She has studied the architecture of a foreign object until it stories to her hands. It has taken an entire year. She has made thumbnail drawings of everything. Little drawings like words pepper her head. She thinks of nothing else.

When her mother first fled she asked, "Where is my father?" And her mother said, "You don't have a father anymore. There are more important things in life than fathers. Remember that."

If she put it back together it would not take a year, since she's learned its making. But she will not put it back together. She didn't do it in order to put it back together. She did it for the drawings. And photographs—she photographs the dismembered bodies and tacks them up on the wall. All the parts are represented. She plans a burial in the dusty land near her house—metallic corpse parts. Rows of dead machines. Fuck technology, she thinks to herself, I'll make land mines made from potatoes.

10. national security

The first component of war in _____ and in the wars in _____ for the U.S. was an aerial attack on the civilian infrastructure, targeting power, sewage, and water systems; that is, a form of biological warfare, designed to ensure long-term suffering and death among civilians so that the U.S. would be in a good position to attain its political goals for these regions. This is not war; rather, state terrorism. (Noam Chomsky).

11. world war

The police were aware that I had comrades who were hiding in F. and who were due to arrive in S. to carry out certain operations. They knew enough to know that I knew about their travels so they made me phone them and tell them it was good to come now. They came by boat. Near the shore, the police attacked them. They shined searchlights and killed all of them, there on the shore. There were five people in the boat, all men. Two died instantaneously and three jumped into the water. One of those survived and is now imprisoned.

I killed five men that day. I mean I killed five men face to face. That is the only thing I have ever done in my life that seems unbearable, that is the difficult part of staying alive. Living with those murders. I gave the signal to the men in the boat. I was there; an eyewitness. No, not an eyewitness. I was tied hand and foot by rope in the car, and after I gave the signal with a light the policeman pulled me down hard. I heard the shooting.

At the trial the police said there were no witnesses, that it had been an armed attack and they had responded in self-defense. That is why we have our own newspaper, because when someone is found dead with their feet burned to charred stubs, we will print a photo and an explanation. The national news media prints the government's press releases and police statements. A photo from the knees up, a suicide.

What will you print? How will you tell these stories?
You are a very curious woman. Do you have children?
Not very many women in the organization have children.
Are you afraid? What makes you afraid? I've read all about
your wars. You tell wonderful stories, don't you? You are
particularly skilled at telling stories, I think.

96

from The Boy Stories

Johnny Depp in *What's Eating Gilbert Grape*
For the longest goddamn time I've been imagining
the same picture. It eats at me bone-side-in and without
rest. I've got this ache—dull and void and so familiar I
can't recognize it—about the gap between being and *being.* You know? Christ. I don't know what I'm talking
about.

I had these moments when we were together. Scenes,
yeah, but something else was fucking going on. I mean
it. For example, that water tower scene. You know the
one, where Arnie has to climb when he's emotionally
tweaked. We'd climb, me after him, him looking down
at me. Scene after scene. Chasing Leonardo. A strain of
small muscle at the neck. An ache in the squinted eye
looking up. It would hit. Like a bullet...like a razor in
the center of my skull it would hit: this is not fiction.
This is not a movie. With each hand over hand rung to
rung and looking up and partly sky but not and the
goddamn camera eye following I'd be thinking, this is
real. This is what it is to be me climbing after a fucking
face. And that bellowing of Leonardo being Arnie was

just a cacophonous exclamation point; he was not Arnie, in that he fucking *was* and it was too much accurate. All the me being me and him being him and mirrors and the image of myself staring back at myself...my God Leonardo is so goddamn beautiful and him being Arnie like a terrible inversion—too perfect.

What do I say to me? My role. The "caretaker" brother of an overburdened family. But the inside-out of it is me looking up, chasing a beautiful boy like chasing a life, always a bit behind, always in danger of smacking my own life silly across the jaw or a woman or a motel room or an image. Me chasing a beautiful boy.

Fucker. In the scene I hold him out of the bathtub. Me holding a shivering beautiful boy. I wrestle him out of a tree onto the ground. Me wrestling a beautiful boy. He was gone from me before me. Lips. Eyes. Jaw. Tabloid texts of my life like a script. Me following the script of me. Easy to play a man ripping up from the inside toward the desire of boy. Not beautiful.

Do you want this face? Fuck if you do. And I do; that's the failing.

Harvey Keitel in *Bad Lieutenant*

His spine and his cock and his abdomen and the crazy small of his back make a scream up the torso of his man and his throat and his mouth and his lips and his skull dull ache scream of a man his voice but not the voice of a man but his animal. And his pouring transparent liquor and his shooting transparent liquid and his arm and his gut and his unflinching addiction close face his too big his close-up his enlarged face his engorged cock his too much his.

The sound.

John Malkovich in *Dangerous Liaisons*

I have always known I had a superior intellect as contrasted with most of the incredible idiocy of those around me. This is not arrogance. It is survival, it is learned behavior in the most classical sense. For instance. Most husks of human walk around on a daily basis speaking with wisdom about things they haven't the tiniest microscopic inkling about, from the standpoint of experience or even the gray folds surrounding skull; they speak and speak and words pour out of the holes in their faces, endless blather so that, in the end, they are not even close to human. They are babbling skulls. Yak-cracking their jaws. Let me talk to you about the much misunderstood word, "contempt." In a way, it is the underbelly of another greatly misperceived word in our seemingly ordered language, "beauty." One cannot approach such words without sublime, chaotic heart throb and yet most do with the unbelievably casual monotony of a cow's jaw circularly grinding its grass. There are many ways to phrase the despised; however, I myself prefer bitter scorn. The phrase carries with it an economy of sound and tune that merits much. An even better version: derision. Listen to the sound. One need not struggle for meaning, for understanding. Pure phonetic precision.

During shooting, which I turn back on as a phrase and ask that you turn back on for a moment only, a glance, "during shooting," and ask is that not the most exquisite phrase, no, not the phrase, break it down again, the word alone, "shooting," to mean, not the bullet from the chamber at all, but rather the shot from the lense, the machinery, the vivid technological wonder of organs without a body producing the image of bodies moving in light and small squares…violent laughter. Digression. Give me pardon. Words convulse me without permission in a thousand different ways. During shooting. The scene wherein Glenn Close is describing her "upbringing," and again, the word "upbringing," but to move to the point, her face; she speaks of stabbing a fork into her thigh to discipline herself in a world where women are objects (*Then*, eh? Never now, correct?), small monologue, and I am seated next to her, lascivious, the broken frame of courtly. Do not miss the point. Her eyes. Her mouth. The eyes glaze over as if in dream or sex or opium (you will forgive me, of the *times*). Did you see her face? Not the words. And I

99

am telling you that this is "contempt" and "beauty" miraculously and yet accurately conflated into one.

Do not misinterpret me; I am not praising a fellow actor or gushing over her work. I am pointing out to you, you who sit in the dark eating popcorn and doing whatever it is that you do in your small lives during the light hours, and especially those of you who think yourselves intellectual, those of you who feign contemporary forms of knowledge with martini-handed glitz—I am telling you that this image, this face of hers (and the words too but more specifically the face), as I have related it to you, the glaze of the eyes, the mouth parting its lips only slightly and yet cavernously, this. My most present self. I. Violent head with its obscene holes spewing.

It had nothing to do with her. With the "part." With her "role" or her "monologue" or the "shot." It was me, I tell you, perfectly distilled into image. My cock surrendered itself to its hardness. An Aubrey Beardsley illustration. I fucked myself. The cusp, the in-between, the line of nothing: contempt, beauty.

Al Pacino in *Dog Day Afternoon* thinking about *The Godfather*

His thoughts roll inside his skull like dice in a cup. It's the goddamndest thing. The effeminate side of Michael. He hadn't brought it to consciousness before now, but now it grows as an image magnified to cinematic proportions. The lips. The eyes. The face next to violence. His rage. Like the cunt of an icon pulled open, those pre-Christian stone relics—life in death and death in life. Violence is a woman, this is the reason men inflict violence against women. He nearly doubles over with laughter, the crew looks him over strangely but not with alarm. No one wanted him for that part except Coppola. Everyone thinks he will be perfect in this part. He knows the director saw something, but until now, he hadn't an idea in hell what it had been.

This man who robs banks in the name of love, in the name of metamorphoses from man to woman…. This man is out of time. The film is out of time. The decade is not the time. The character, the actor. None of them in time. He must bend the body out of time, the mouth, the eyes, the physical presence out of time. It is violence and it is not violence. It is desire out of proportion, beyond Marilyn and toward some other, mutable loving body, some other director not yet born, some other actor bleeding beyond the square of the screen into vision.

He sees it. He can touch it with his tongue. The tenderness he has felt all along inhabiting this character fills his mouth as saliva and surges in his veins as blood begging release.

He is not a woman.

Harvey Keitel in *The Piano*

"I was very affected by Tungia, the woman playing Hira in the film. She came down to Karekare beach, and the first thing she did was cross the beach to the sea, bend over and sprinkle herself with water. And I said, 'What are you doing?' And she said, 'I'm asking the sea to welcome me.'"

Linda Hunt in *The Year of Living Dangerously*

hand and hand pounding he is not me he is not like me hand drum hand pound to key to key to finger type black out taut click to black in dreams in dreams i saw him i breathed him he brought me he bore me to life to live is dreaming drumming do i want to cut to black to key cut me my life done pounding to hands my hands is this sweet sleep pushing in delirium oh her early in morning her pearling skin her skin soaked with rain her face fire film for anything i would give anything to give her to him i give her to him hands and under and pounding drum me i give her to him he to her running and dreaming and body and body and wet and turn to key to cut to shot crack wicked will the will of the body is dizzy to desire desire's lengthening dream thick with wet and sleep and ending in hands desiring hands dulled and delirious and drumming in dull is it sky...is it sky...these no longer mine...hands.

Michael Madsen in _Reservoir Dogs_

Some weird fucking shit. I mean think about it. I love the guy but he's fucking insane, man. Guys sitting around intellectually musing about the fuck-factor in Madonna's "Like a Virgin". A guy torturing some poor fuck with gasoline, cutting his goddamn ear off, and dancing in some quasi-jovial prance in a warehouse listening to jack-shit 70s tunes...white shirt. Black pants. Fucking metal for brains (Laughter; deep and wide and sexy). Man, I love these guys. Tarantino. Oliver Stone. Sick fucks!! But necessary, understand? Otherwise we'd be swimming in Jell-O. Know what I mean? I'm just fucking glad they're around in my round. I mean that scene was a motherfucking _gas_ to play.

Tim Roth in _Reservoir Dogs_

He makes this sound, Keitel, a sort of wail, but all crumpled up like his heart is...you know when you wad up a piece of paper and throw it out? That's how I picture his heart. When he makes that sound. Right before he blows me away, there at the end, where all the men are dead except us.

Steve Buscemi in _Reservoir Dogs_

"Why do I have to be Mr. Pink?"

Woody Allen in _Husbands and Wives_

Judy Davis was brilliant. And I'll tell you why she was brilliant. There's a scene when she's out on her first date, some poor schmuck, a real nice guy, wants to take her to see _Don Giovanni_, and her face and her body are so supremely twitchy and white like a knuckled fist. She moves around the room with this electricity that sparks and flies off of objects, tables, the couch. She moves down the hall like neuroses embodied and there is this other her that's following her down the hall like a second self, watching, whispering "don't go, don't do it, retract, return, turn back," but the first self is too far and fast and picking up the phone and dialing his number and holding that earring in her hand so in sync with her out-of-control arms and legs and head and mouth. I mean really, just exquisite. I thought I might...might...I don't know what, vomit or something, projectile heave. You don't instruct someone how to do that. You point and wave from the shadows like some inconsequential bird and hope that you don't make some awful squawking noise when you speak.

I've just been so lucky in these years to have crossed paths with such extraordinary women. Like an accident of the stars, really.

Marlon Brando in *Apocalypse Now*
"The horror...the horror."

Rutger Hauer in *Blade Runner*

Is history a death's head, as a man in exile once wrote? I have been a cyborg, a new Aryan, blue-eyed white haired demi-god in these months. Even now my body is changing. This is the last time I will be awarded a role based on this body. Already the prometheus bends toward his falling. Muscles atrophy. The sublime moment on the mountain struck dead after the glimpse. Perhaps it is not the body. Perhaps it is something to do with the hands, or something to do with the gray folds of brain, an attempt to fold and turn and push back all of living.

The monster beheld is beautiful, these men of our own making, these things of darkness, put together in parts, arms, legs, heads, eyes, his bicep, his jaw, his abdomen. My God.

I see clearly that we have no history, none of us, we are made and unmade by the simplest of gestures, by a body leaving a frame outdoing a body leaving a room, by two hands maginified to cinematic proportions making you forget what hands do. The nail in the hand to keep back death. To remember Christ. To echo a monster. To forget a man.

Robert De Niro in *Taxi Driver*
"You talkin' to me?"

Nick Cage in *Leaving Las Vegas*

You know I read that *fucking* script until my eyes burned back through my skull. I kept thinking of this line from Celine: "grub ich mich in dich und in dich" and their meaning: "I burrow into you and into you." Crazy, huh. I don't know what my *problem* was entering the text. If you can't bore down into the text's layers you are *fucked*, you are one sorry-ass sack of shit. The thing kept staring back at me with a coldness that really gave me the heebie-jeebies.

It's like I've been cast as a *witness* or some goddamn thing like that. Like I can't rest into the voice or the action or the motivations or the character at all, like I'm hovering over it all like a *second self*. Like the whole scene collapses the moment I try to enter. The goddamn script's remains laugh up at me like old ashes from a burned out butt.

Or it's like a knot, a four-way knot made of all the things in life we retreat from, destruction, death, desire, doubt. Maybe I need a fucking *shrink* to get through this thing. Or maybe I need to shut off thinking all at once. Act. The *body*, mindless.

What's agonizing is the simplicity of this guy's movements. Everytime I try it, for instance, on the patio, today, it's too *campy*. Like I'm camping everything up, cheating with flair and style. That's it. There is no style here. Bare bones or something.

It's catastrophic, this unyielding page after page slapping my reading my mind my body around. There is danger and yet it's laughable, it's all silly and drunk and jumping around in the most comic of shadows. What is the source, I keep asking myself to *get at the center*, you know, down to it, the nitty gritty.

On the tenth day it hits me *like lightning*, like the moment itself. Mutation. The concept of mutation. If I can read with a sense of sentences and thoughts shifting their frames like blurred images or speeded up and lagged sound I can see this guy emerging and retreating, in and out of focus, in and out of action, there and gone, there and gone. Mutation, mutable, not a character at all. As yet unfinished image/sound/voice/gesture. And I *dig* this notion because it forgets and un-remembers everything that is supposed to *work* in acting, you know man, everything that is supposed to give *form* and *function* and balls to the whole shebang.

Sean Penn in *Carlito's Way*
Nuyoricans and Jews, Spics, Wops, Kikes. Fucking melting pot's a crock. We all are what we are. We love each other through hate in these neighborhoods. That's love too, motherfucker. That's love too.

Ving Rhames in *Pulp Fiction*
"My nigger."

Spike Lee in *Do the Right Thing*
I go to a Knicks game and what I'm thinking is, yeah, motherfucker, you got your Jew and your niggah directors all lined up for viewing. Isn't that just America all over? I don't make movies. You do.

Jack Nicholson in *One Flew Over the Cuckoo's Nest*
What I want is the perfect moment. The opening in the game where physical violence turns into beauty. Truth. Animal force brought to art, the ball rising and falling through sweat and ether like a moon. What I want is the blow smashing the glass into a thousand pieces, the head, the elbow, the shoulders like weapons butting open a skull to blood, everything stylized and taken to cinematic proportions, everyone drinking beer out of plastic cups and screaming, their mouths garish and spilling, like a fucking Roman spectacle.

Chuck Palahniuk talking to Lidia Yuknavitch about Brad Pitt talking to Chuck Palahniuk about *Fight Club*
So I'm sitting there baking in the sun in one of those director's chairs you always imagine are lining the sets, and they are, man, they *are* lining the sets, and I'm kinda

105

YUKNAVITCH

Lidia

hot and this guy next to me is telling me all about the book because he doesn't know I wrote the book. And I'm actually fascinated by what he's saying about the book, fascinated enough that at one point I actually start seeing what he means, his angle begins to overtake the actual act of writing the thing. Just then there is some kind of commotion on the set. I see the crowds, the cameramen and other workers buzz and jolt, I see them as an organism breaking apart. It sounds like fuck suddenly instead of a movie being constructed and colors whir and blitz and the organism parts like a sea and it's Brad, he's running a line through them. And he looks like complete crap because it's far enough into the shooting that they've got

106 him looking like crap, you know, his face all fucked up and so forth. But he looks even wild-eye wicked worse than that, I mean he looks like one crazy motherfucking bat-out-of-hell, and it's then I realize that he's running straight for us, no, straight for me. I'll be honest with you, I sort of gripped the arms of the director's chair and braced myself, I could feel the muscles in my jaw tighten even though I was smiling. I was sitting there thinking, he's gonna fucking come right at me, he's gonna fucking tackle me, but he stops hot short right in front of me, a little cloud of dirt-dust rising around his feet. His breath is jacknifed in his lungs and his face is nearly flying off. He leans down in that heavy breathing and his face is in mine and he grabs my shoulders, my shoulders rising a little up to meet his hands, and he says, "Thank you for writing this fucking part. This is the best fucking part I've ever had in my life." And he releases me and takes off running the way he came, back, through, a man written alive, I guess.

John Travolta in *Pulp Fiction*

The whole thing was funnier than shit the entire time. No lie. Every scene. For example, the overdose scene. We were laughing so hard I thought I was gonna blow snot all over her, or accidentally stab her through the heart. Earlier, when Eric said, "prank caller prank caller" I nearly shit my pants, just the tone of his voice, right? Mr. pot-smoking, wear your bathrobe all day, eat cereal for dinner paranoid-boy. But when he said "you bring the needle down in a stabbing motion" and he does this sort of *Psycho* move up and down with the syringe, me and Uma nearly choked laughing. He just got so into it. He just fucking kicked ass. That whole panic-what-the-fuck serious-as-hell-guy thing. Stoltz, man. Man alive. I swear. That was so fucking funny. That whole overdose scene. We had to shoot it like a billion times.

Kenneth Branagh in *Hamlet*
I honestly thought about playing more than one part, you know, for effect and affect.

Kevin Spacey in *American Beauty*
I don't want to be alive in any other time.

Jackson Pollack on James Dean in *East of Eden*
There will never be a male actor again like him. He was not an actor. The closest thing is Brando. But in him we reached a kind of Zenith, and it will never come again. In him we had a chance to see what a man is. That dissolution. Vulnerability, or brute force. Shaking a body to its bone. No, it is more than that. It is about the medium of film, too. He was pure movement. Like particle physics in the shape of a man. He bled the screen. He inverted the whole motion of the picture.

Beauty

All life is the disease of matter.
—Goethe

Allegory is the projection of the metaphoric axis of language onto its metonymic, or temporal dimension.
—Craig Owens

We write in order to forget our foreknowledge of the total opacity of words and things, or, perhaps worse, because we do not know whether things have or do not have to be understood.
—Paul de Man

Beauty had a tumor pulsing just behind her brain, near the left earlobe, near the surface of the skin. As skull bulges go it was not remarkable. She had a naked flayed head from the chemo with a few sparse almost-hairs hanging on, and the little knob of disease stuck out just a little further than her ear. Her skin shone colors drawn from the probing needles, pain-killers, drugs and radiation—red to blue to gray to purple, as if her veins were leaking. This being her seventh illness she had learned to accompany her diseases with the warm browns and liquefactious surrenders of whiskey, a medicine which had outlived doctors, patients and death. She had yellowish eyes that gleamed like bourbon marbles inside their little sockets from the slow, faithful submergence of her liver into pickled oblivion. One of her eyes wouldn't stay put either, it wandered, it floated untethered from the tendons meant to hold organs in place. Beauty was also lopsided. One of her legs was four inches shorter than the other, the result of the defect called birth. She had a piece of steel in her hip where bone ought to bear weight. And then there was the mass of sinewy fibers in her chest which had metastasized until her breasts blew off. It seems at first she had had a chance, from the outside everything looked normal, but when they finally got a look inside it was like a new colony, a world, a universe hiding just beneath the mams. So off they went and now she carried zippered flesh from shoulder to shoulder. The nurses in the chemo lab had begun to think of her as a real character, because every time she came in, something else was broken, bleeding, peeling, melting, oozing.

Lastly, bad uterus. The Dow-Con Shield fiasco had left just a hollowed out tunnel which she assumed if you peered into you would see all the way up her esophagus to Cincinnati. Luckily, she had made enough off of the settlement to help pay for ever expanding medical care.

Clip-clap, clip-clap, clip-clap. This was the sound of her footsteps, heavy on the clap. As if some dissonant, out-of-whack orchestra racked out a beat only she heard. Bud-clip-clap, bud-clip-clap-bud, bud-clip-clap—sometimes she used a cane. If Beauty was walking behind you, this is what you would hear. If Beauty was walking toward you, here is what would be in your head: just look

109

down. Feign existence. Just go limp. There is a thick bubble of invisible surrounding me. There is a buffer of nothing.

Truth is, you couldn't really call her a woman at all, except for this: Beauty was pregnant and she owned a TV.

The only thing Beauty knew more about than illness was human drama. Illness put her in front of the TV, the magazine, the book and the movie so many times that she knew true human drama like the back of her hand. In fact, she had made big bucks off *Reader's Digest*—she sent them a story they couldn't refuse about how a merry band of hobos had rescued a man who had his legs severed from a passing train. Three hundred bucks a pop for half-human people who survived floods, car wrecks, fires and worse. She had a whole trunkful of made for TV movie scripts. Like brothers and sisters tucked away in a coffin she'd given a face to every misery on earth.

About the pregnancy. Initially she had considered the same question you probably would in her position: why me, how me, I mean, the rule is, bad uterus, no wall for the growth to cling to, no glow, no joy, just ovaries hanging around dropping eggs like pellets for chickens. But "why me" had become such a mighty roar of ridiculous laughter for Beauty that the questions just came out like farts now. Too many beans, not enough roughage. It never occurred to her to ask, from where, from whom. Some questions had already bled out of her brain forever. Anyway, she just wasn't dying like they said she would. So she quit chemo hoping the belly bulge would beat the tumor. Seemed logical. Remission and Conception both had three syllables a piece. You could trust words that way. You could say words out loud to yourself and empty them out.

She had to get some fast money for the kid's future, even though she wasn't necessarily convinced she would die, since instead of dying so far she had only multiplied diseases, mishaps and unfortunate circumstances. The phone had been DC'd, the TV only produced ghost-like images of figures barely recognizable through the thick snow (luckily she had each day's lineup memorized), the radio hovered between Mahler and static messages floating between waves. She was beginning to loose control of her bladder as well.

Now then.

Near-corpse that she was, she knew enough to know that this, I mean her story, would make a superb TV drama. Between 6:00 and 9:00 p.m. Monday through Friday and especially on Sunday the TV was filled to the brim with the walking dead of human dramas: the sick the slow the criminal the crazy the evil the loveless the psycho the decrepit the unborn the born-too-early the born-too-late the left for dead born. It was this last category which interested her. Lately she had noticed a surge of programs on babies and children left by unfit mothers in various refuse sights, dungeons, abandoned Buicks, alleys and shrubbery. So a uterus-less, tumor-headed, breastless, cancerous, lopsided, burned-out pregnant woman might have a shot in there somewhere. On the other hand, she was not a stupid woman, and she knew that they would never believe her actual story, so what would they buy? She knew from writing the hobo story that pathos was the key—it didn't matter what had really happened, it only mattered that people could eat it up. She realized she had to think of a more clever story than hers, one with a hook, something to draw them in. The question was, how to present a pathos worthy of TV attention. The tumor made all her ideas roll around in her head like dice in a cup.

III

Meanwhile strange, anonymous stirrings. The joining of cells lethal to both. The slow roll of an enclosed wave taking shape. The curling of water around organic material. The belly turning cave. The spine rearranging. The nauseous love up the throat. The slow bend of a body toward carrying life.

She took a train to Hollywood in order to sell a story. On the way to Hollywood she kept drinking to think of a story, and what came out as the title was *The Train to*

Nacogdoches. She had considered just plain *Train* but she
loved the sound of the word Nacogdoches and her mother
had been born there anyway. She wrote the word "synopsis" at the top of a yellow legal pad turned on its side.
The word "synopsis" banked off the edge of her skull.
Three syllables. She liked that. She might have to replace
"Zoel Weiker," the words she repeated to herself for sheer
sound pleasure with "synopsis." Underneath "synopsis"
she wrote:

> Woman named Sara hears a low voice in
> the desert. While pulled over on the side
> of the road in a baby-blue Buick because
> of a busted radiator Sara is told by this
> low voice in the desert that she is going
> to be with child. Sara says my ass, I'm 53
> years old, and the voice says, haven't you
> been watching television lately? Post-
> menopausal women are conceiving all
> over the place. Sara spends the rest of the
> story shifting through denial gears as her
> belly grows and her Buick miraculously
> cures itself. She ends up meeting many
> magical people out in the desert (mostly
> Indians and other outcasts) and with love,
> tenderness and wisdom places the new-
> born in a box-car headed for Nacogdoches.
> A toothless old veteran train-hopper
> named Zibby smiles her gums and waves
> a three-fingered hand as the train pulls
> away.

She thought it was a good start but she knew there
had to be more to it than that for the TV guys and anyway, American audiences needed to feel bad and good at
the same time so she had to deal with that too. She decided to wait for more of the story to show up in a dream.
*Meanwhile the need to sleep on her side over-
takes her in the night. The cramping and*

uncramping of legs stretching, devolving, limbs longing to travel back before bipedalism. The warm ache between the thighs not for sex but more than that. The wet secretions. The night- mare visions of infants with pig's tales and fangs and the ears of a blue-blooded hound.

She needed to get back to what she knew, back to the inner-workings of TV and biology. The way cancer breeds. The way channels flip people into images and stories which fit into sequential abstracts waiting for ratings and time-slots. The way the tragic yawns after it is told too many times. The way a body sinks into the cupped hands of a sofa-chair and eats human. She thought about her TV. She pictured the picturetube. The television was indeed dys-functional right now, but she knew what was in there. Be-hind the picture tube, behind the lie of fuzzy-nothings was Montel Williams. 10:00 a.m. meant Montel. She knew that like she knew "the back of her hand," a phrase she liked, and now she looked at the backs of her hands and they looked like, well, the back of skinless and textured wood. What did she know about the backs of her hands? And she looked again, because there of course must be something vital, something to "know like the back of her hand" or else people wouldn't say that. She held her hand out in front of her and tried to picture her television as a divided image between her fingers. On the TV between her out-stretched little twig fingers she knew the whole world was filled with wonderfully abnormal stories of transvestites and strippers and tax fraud men who wore women's panties and junkies and alcoholics whose faces had to be artificially smudged, digitalized or darkened and famous incest survi-vors and mothers who murdered and daughters who held school cafeterias filled with pimply slobbering momma's boys at gun point. And the Montel questions, the micro-phones, the caller being there, the audience raising their hands and probing like the blind nub-heads of earthworms. She put herself in the guest's chair. She talked the talk.

"How long has it been?"

"Years. Days. I don't remember. I'm supposed to be dead."

"And the pain, has it been very difficult?"

"Well, there are muscles, tendons, ligaments, as you can imagine. There are organs ripping me from the inside out. You know, you learn to live with it."

"Of course."

"I'm talking about a slow disintegration. Over time. Not something you can understand from the outside."

"Is there anything of substance left? Anything productive?"

"It's not a matter of flesh and bones. There isn't really a medical term for it. I find a better, more accurate description to be, lace. Imagine delicate lace-flesh, blood, corpuscles and the tissue consuming itself. An inside-out. Leaves and dung on a compost heap. Fertilizer. Fer—ti—li—zer."

An audience member or a Caller.

"Where do you get your spiritual strength?"

The most pukey question imaginable. How did any human being ever develop the voice of human drama when some other idiot was out there asking that, hacking away, severing limbs? Her answer: "What's the matter with death?" She looked out the window of the train at the dizzy blur of land and sky.

She moved on to a consideration of setting. This Sara wasn't in just any desert, it had to be a symbolic thing, The Desert, a desert of deserts. She decided to invent a desert named "Crab" in Arizona and to give Sara cancer of the uterus, so that she would be dying but only a little bit and so the new life would have to pass through non-life on its way out. She drew this picture to indicate where the Great Crab Desert was in relation to the black dome of night, just under the Northern Hemisphere between Leo and Gemini:

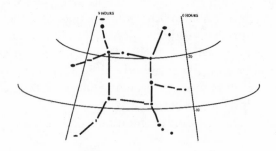

She gave a short description of the Great Crab Desert.
She put her hand on her belly.

*That region, that great sand body expanse of
rise and fall and gentle gestures rolling in and
on themselves. The push of sky and wind
against the belly of land. The land arguing up
to join them. Portrait barren, the giving and
taking, the murderous love of land that sweeps
reptilian and thorny extremes to sleep. The force
of a handless fist. Waterless belligerent. Unin-
habitable Fruitless. Lonely longing movable
hills exchanging grains for molecules of air. The
cupping of empty ness. The horizonless vision.
Desertum. The Abandon. Now that was a
desert.*

Beauty put her pen down and began vomiting blood.
Her nose ran, her bladder spilled, her eyes flooded. Even
the wax in her ears felt as if it was melting, dripping
slowly through the canals. When the train stopped and
some men came to wipe her up and away, she kept saying I'm sorry. I'm sorry. Forgive me. Terrible. No control. Manuscript. Am writing. Anything with three syllables.

The story sold, but a lot happened in between.

Somewhere in between the train and the delivery she
realized that Sara needed to be black, a liar, crazy; hear-
ing voices or in prison, that the baby she had to leave
the baby because "God told her to do it." The characters
in the story and the images on the screen of poor unwed
and unfit mothers and whiskey drinking girls with
flames shooting out of their hair, all the mothers who
abandoned children and all the intimate forgottens
formed a new desert tribe, a community of cripples and
crazies that are the waste material of all human drama.
So it turns out that Sara dies. But through her train-hop-
ping daughter Sara becomes a desert myth. Possible syn-
dication. Sara the moving woman in the Blue Buick the
woman who moves through all the pieces of land and
keeps the desert tied to its own arms, legs, eyes. The myth

115

of Sara in the desert:
Someone in the desert busts a radiator.
Someone is disturbed by the beauty of it.
Someone is wrecking the grammar.
Someone is too big for the house.
Someone is dying on a slow train to Nacogdoches.
Someone jumped the labor.
Someone cries the sweet airless night.
Someone a woman tired and slowly.
Someone put a nickel in at the spine.
Someone believed it was like this.
Someone soft a prayer.
Someone frightened of the sounds at the door.
Someone lets the animals in.
Someone flips the channel.
Someone opens body.
Someone likes to watch.
Someone alone a lonely.
Someone fades away.
Someone leaves the empty.
Someone enters the crowded box of undesirables.

Of course Beauty was re-hospitalized. The tumor was throbbing and the bladder thing turned strange; it was as if her belly and abdomen were imploding, turning back toward her spine, reaching for vertebrae senselessly. She tried Kegels, squeezing her little lips and muscles for all she was worth, but nothing helped. So it was back to the big house and the little beds, the tubes and needles and machinery meant to give life surrounding her like armies of metallic and plastic aliens. The mucous going out of the cavities through one tube. The fluid coming through the layered membranes through another. Tube life.

They discovered that they had to go back inside, through the gut this time. Premature, Beauty thought. This was it.

Meanwhile, in the too-white light of the operating room. Underneath the knives. Masked hazy figures in and out of vision. Beauty dreamed the story of Sara in the desert. Just before the masked ones slipped the blade in cold and slit a crevasse inside Beauty's mound of belly she dreamed Sara in the desert. Just as they pulled the milk-blue globe of a cantaloupe-sized tumor from her barren womb, she delivered. And what a delivery: the pilot went series. The series to feature film. THX. Sensurround. Meryl Streep in the lead—no make-up—like when she was in *Ironweed*. Haggard. I hear she's up for an Academy Award.

Truth is, Beauty's dead.

117

YUKNAVITCH

Lidia

Citations of a Heretic

1. Interrogative
(excerpt #13)
Q. When did you last hear the voice speaking to you?
A. Yesterday and today.
Q. At what time did you hear it yesterday?
A. I heard it three times: once in the morning, once at the hour of retreat, and the third time in the evening at the hour of the Ave Maria. Very often I hear it more frequently than I tell you.
Q. What were you doing when you heard it yesterday morning?
A. I was asleep, and the voice woke me.
Q. Did it wake you by touching your arm?
A. It woke me without touching me.
Q. Are the said saints, Saint Catherine and Saint Margaret dressed alike?
A. I will not tell you anything more about them now; I am not allowed to.
Q. Are they of the same age?
A. I am not allowed to say.

Q. How do you know that it is Saint Catherine and Saint Margaret who talk to you?

A. I have told you often enough that they are Saint Catherine and Saint Margaret—believe me if you like.

Q. Do you always see them in clothes?

A. I have always seen them in the same shape, their heads very richly crowned.

Q. In what shape do you see them?

A. I see their faces.

Q. Have they any hair?

A. C'est bon a savoir!

Q. Is their hair long and hanging down?

A. I do not know. I do not know whether they have any arms or other members.

Q. If they had no members, how could they speak?

A. How is it that you speak?

Q. Answer the question.

A. I refer that to God.

Q. What did Saint Michael look like when he appeared to you?

A. I did not see any crown, and I know nothing of his garments.

Q. Was he naked?

A. Do you think he should be clothed?

Q. Had he any hair?

A. Why should it have been cut off?[1]

> One has to speak with thunder
> and heavenly fireworks to feeble
> and dormant senses. But the
> voice of beauty speaks softly:
> it steals into only the most
> awakened souls.[2]

Not that her voice did not dip and curve between these two, torturing us with the truths we forced on her. Even now I am struck by the extraordinary irony of a woman speaking about disembodied voices to the invisible Body

---

[1] 100100
[2] 010100

which is the Tribunal. Voices touching voices is stunning to me, considering the stakes. I first witnessed the RE-ANIMATION sequence of the trial of Saint Jeanne d'Arc in 2290, although it was actually the thirtieth such sequence activated on record. This J bore little resemblance to the one of 1431. And yet, at the same time, her countenance, the rigid jaw-line, the black, sunken eyes, the shaven head with the Rebel scarifications decorating her scalp, her dead stare into the black emptiness of the arena—all these re-membered an earlier vision of that first woman. Magnificent. Had the Tribunal created her themselves they could not have given her a more perfectly repetitive body, a more perfect beauty.

120
> Shamash the glorious sun
> endowed him with beauty,
> adad the god of the storm
> endowed him with courage,
> the great gods made his
> beauty perfect, surpassing
> all others, terrifying[3]...

Legends reproduce immortality quite truthfully. Butterflies in clouds accompanied her standard; pigeons miraculously fluttered toward her; men fell into rivers and were drowned; dead babies yawned and came to life; flocks of little birds perched on bushes to watch her making war.[4] Could this not be said of the figure before us now, in all her stubborn and radiant defiance? Had she not inspired thousands of rebels to collect and dream of erasing us from eternity, freedom, materiality without tyranny? Yes, most of all she re-membered the farthest gone, the longest forgotten, sunk into memory and words. A woman who took up arms against the powers over her, a woman dressed like a man, J who called herself

> la Pucelle, lair, pernicious,
> deceiver of the people, sorceress,
> superstitious blasphemer,

[3] 001100
[4] 100100

presumptuous, disbeliever in the
faith, boastful, idolatrous, cruel,
dissolute, invoker of devils, apostate,
schismatic and heretic.[5]

The distance? The gap between the accused and the accusers, as in all of history, is characterized by living flesh
and blood on the one hand and ethereal systems on the
other, pathetic systems sick with the decay of progress
and power. If only there truly were a way to go back and
forget. Forget the rituals which took the material and broke
its back in the name of law in the first place.

Remorse? Dead for us except in traces of desire and
nostalgia. Today this play between the flesh and the airy
system of penal governance is as literally true as it could
ever be. For them, the residual wholly human who are
the Rebel Survivors, memory is mysterious and vague but
also a lifeline to a breathable past. Imagine! A past that
one has lived and died in and for. A past recollected in the
living matter, in cells and pores and cytoplasmic movements. The journey of neurons. The living dream.

For us, it is the very force of a life we can never retrieve. REANIMATION is our only claim left on the material world—the grasping and clawing backwards toward the idea of the past is all the humanness we have
left in us. Greedy, envious angels! We are the effects of a
present, we are the symptoms of a race untethered to any
trace of their own passing. There is no passing without
replaying a human. REANIMATION takes the forces of
the present, the activities, the desires, the gestures, the
human material and activates them with the actuality of
the past. The informational banks stage the present crime.
For the most part we are hovering envy, waiting for the
next transgression to be executed by the lowest class, those
most biologically determined. The Code of Transgression:
the violation of the law,
command, or duty. The

121

[5] 100100

exceeding of due bounds or
limits. To act in violation, to
transgress.[6]

The Code determines which events are punishable. The accused are guilty at once and relegated to the Forum, an arena wherein history is REANIMATED from the records and the newly accused are forced to become players. The use of screens is essential for the player. Reels and reels have been collected and restored in order to ensure verisimilitude. The player is issued an historically accurate script. The player cannot become fatigued or emotionally distraught as she recites the script. Occasionally there are attempts at intellectual escape, fictions woven in between lines, but the screens aid in fixing the object of the history within the drama.

122

How the players play is not very consistent. Some of the women are bad actors, and so they are pathetically reduced to mimicry and mime with bits of pleading here and there; like so many idiotic parrots fluttering and screeching. These are of little use to us. They are killed quickly—the rush is quick and fades immediately. But there are those few who rise like struggling, wrestling angels to meet the voice and corpus of their past, and in an irreducibly physical clash they shake the stage with an echo which surpasses the thing itself. . . and the rapture is sublime.

The J was one of those.

It matters little what has actually occurred—a little more or less like history, makes no difference. All their transgressions serve to produce the material for these scenes, so that we, divorced from human, can *feel* corporeality.

Trials have evolved forward and backward at the same time. The Romans would delight in our little plays, I am sure. This is not the examination of evidence and applicable law by a competent jury to determine the issue of

[6] 110100

specified charges or claims. This is closer to a state of pain or anguish caused by a difficult situation or condition:
> The fiery trial through
> which we pass.[7]

and the executions deal directly with performance. You see, to execute, to act, to perform. Trials are chosen based on the category of activity of the accused. REANIMATION serves to recollect any cerebral fragmentation caused by individual human and psychic disturbances. All stories bleed into one. Scapegoats, as archaic as they seem, serve a vital function in a society which has lost the idea of a human soul and the body containing it.

It was bad for her from the beginning, and yet, quite horribly beautiful. She had no chance, she was

> simply arrested and thrown
> into the world of the trial
> without escape—you can't go
> out, you are arrested—we
> are not authorized to tell
> you that. Go to your room
> and wait there. Proceedings
> have been instituted against
> you, and you will be informed
> of everything in due course.[8]

retrieved unexpectedly, almost by accident. She performed exquisitely. She dug her position profoundly out of the past with such precision it was hard to remember our own present. Her answers made the case against her perfectly, as perfectly as they had in history. She didn't look at the script once. But more astonishing than that and what added to the eroticism of her role was her stealing script from other histories, information the Tribunal is supposed to have exclusive control over! For example, before her first excerpt she transgressed her role with one of the greatest defenses ever recorded.

[7] 101100
[8] 100110

(excerpt #1)

A. How you felt, gentlemen of Athens, when you heard my accusers, I do not know; but I—well, I nearly forgot who I was, they were so persuasive. Yet as for truth—one might almost say they have spoken not one word of truth. But what most astonished me in the many lies they told was that they warned you to take good care not to be deceived by me, "because I was a terribly clever speaker."[9]

It was pure seduction! Something about her voice, her face, her hands reaching out toward us, we all forgot ourselves for an instant. Of course she was eventually interrupted, which took a long second, long enough for her first rupture to register and shake the invisible air in the arena with her murderous speech. The level of courage and intellect needed to have produced such an act is unprecedented. Never has any player stolen material and animated an unauthorized script from one history in order to disrupt the flow of another. Sheer brilliance. It was as if she cited right up and through the expected motion and exploded all consciousness with the deftness of Gods. Like a flash of light she disintegrated the continuum and for one brief moment she was almost a subject, she almost had a gaze which penetrated the empty dark and accused the invisible nothings of their own impotence. Incredible. Driven back to her script she maintained without fail that she saw the Saints with her own eyes, "as surely as the Tribunal." To insist on the reality of hallucinations! The genius of that. We ourselves the apparitions and this girl doubling back into memory and leaping into our present to haunt us with her own, more authentic ghosts. The genius. Socrates himself heard voices.

(excerpt #2)

Q. Do you understand the charges and the sentence against you?

A. I am charged with treason against the State transgressing the Code of Roles for Human Survivors. Beyond this

124

[9] 100011

the validity of my visions is under question. I have been sentenced to death; I am to be burnt at the stake.

Q. Do you admit that you have transgressed your sexual-access role and produced biological offspring with other humans?

A. I am not allowed to answer that.

Q. Do you admit that you frequently cross-dress in order to control sexual-access among the Survivors?

A. I have spoken before on this.

Q. Have the Saints commanded you to refuse to answer certain questions?

A. I have spoken on this. Check the records.[10]

Those apprehended serve two main functions that crystallize both the transgressor's position and our own: the transgressor is punished and brought, at least for an instant before their execution, to the threshold of their beloved human past. History's sweet and lethal moistness touches their tongues as they are guided through the scenes of their beginnings. For us the pleasure of history

> a narrative of events; story.
> A chronological record of
> events, as of the life or
> development of a people or
> institution, often including
> an explanation of or commentary
> on those events. The branch
> of knowledge that records and
> analyzes past events. The events
> forming the subject matter.
> Something that is not of current
> concern. A drama based on
> historical evens. Histora: Gk.:
> learned man.[11]

carries a more drug-like effect; quick and with a burning rush of intellect. We stuff the vicarious thrill, the image, the flesh-word into the black hole of our existences. We

10 111100
11 110110

cannot phenomenologically experience any form of reality per se; we can, however, borrow the experience through theater, and for an instant we can, as they are physically executed, come ecstatically close to that spectacle of death in life which is foreign to us now. The body spasms at the mind's plethora, the mind spasms at the body's excess.

Primary anguish bound up with
sexual disturbances signifies
death. The violence of this
disturbance reopens in the
mind of the man experiencing
it, who also knows what death
is, the abyss that death once
revealed. The violence of death
and sexual violence, when they
are linked together, have this
dual significance. On the one
hand the convulsions of the flesh
are more acute when they are near
to a blackout, and on the other
a blackout, as long as there is
enough time, makes physical pleasure
more exquisite. Mortal anguish
does not necessarily make for
sensual pleasure, but that pleasure is
more deeply felt during mortal anguish.[12]

Like great Gods we are ageless and without comprehension of time and the terminal effect of its "passing" away. These punitive forms are our only experience of memory and the past, and we crave them at all costs. No addiction was ever matched by this. We are such stuff as dreams are made,[13]—the line itself shocks me still. I have understood fully the supreme narcotic. I am the eldest of the Interim Survivors, retaining partial form, eyes, only eyes. I was given consciousness through the Transformation, I stand as the last of those between form and

126

[12] 0101010
[13] 110

non-form, expression and information system, past and the floating nothing we pretend is present. But the Rebels carry the only true seeds of the possibility of life

> the property or quality that
> distinguishes living organisms
> from dead organisms and inanimate
> matter, manifested in functions
> such as metabolism, growth,
> response to stimuli, and reproduction.
> The physical, mental, and spiritual
> experiences that constitute a person's
> existence. The interval of time between
> birth and death; lifetime. The time for
> which something exists in functions. A
> spiritual state regarded as a transcending
> of death. An account of a person's life. A
> source of vitality, animating force. Something
> that actually exists regarded as a
> subject for an artist. Actual reality.[14]

127

since they die inside of their bodies. Sweet word, death. I feel no pity for the woman in the circle of light before us now. My envy is equaled only in intensity by my lust for the small ecstasy that will pass over me.

Burnings are quite popular. They itch the imagination back toward the senses so completely—the smell of fire and flesh, the melting of a face into a dehumanized skull, the shifting of colors as the alchemy surges, the long and exquisite description taking the place of sentencing, pure poetry preceding

> And if someone goes through
> fire for his teaching—what
> does that prove? Truly, it is
> more when one's own teaching
> comes out of one's own burning.[15]

the action.

[14] 111100
[15] 111011

(excerpt # 25)

Q. Since last Thursday (the day of the abjuration), have you heard the voices of Saints Catherine and Margaret?

A. Yes.

Q. What did they say to you?

A. They told me that, through them, God sent me his pity of the betrayal to which I consented in making the abjuration and revocation to save my life, and that in saving my life I was damning myself. Before Thursday, they had told me what I should do, and what I did that day. They told me when I was on the platform that I should answer that preacher boldly; he was a false preacher, and he said I had done several things which I had not done. If I were to say that God had not sent me, I should be damning myself, for it is true that God did send me. My voices have told me, since then, that I did very wrong in doing that which I did, and that I must confess that I did wrong. It was fear of the fire which made me say that which I said.[16]

It took no time at all for the play to become flesh and for us to become giddy with greed for a prolonged journey to the end. I know the disembodied Tribunal was building psychic fervor in anticipation. The greediness of desire

> Now, being naked, to their sordid eyes
> The goodly treasures of nature appeare:
> Which as view with lustful fantasyes,
> Each wisheth to him selfe and to the
> rest enuyes,
> Her yourie necke, her alabaster brest,
> Her paps, which like white silken pillowes were,
> For loue in soft delight thereon to rest;
> Her tender sides, her bellie white and clere,
> Which like an Altar did it selfe uprere,
> To offer sacrifice divine thereon;
> Her goodly thighes, whose glorie did appeare
> Like a triumphall Arch, and thereupon

128

The spoiles of Princes hang'd, which were
the battle won...
Some with their eyes the daintest
morsels chose; Some praise her paps,
some praise her lips and nose;
Some whet their kniues, and strip
their elboes bare[17]

could shatter worlds, were it harnessed as force. The girl
rose to the occasion. No terrified, humble woman subjected to oppression, but a human form whose mouth
flashed out at us when asked to speak on the Gospels that
she would answer nothing but the past truth. She replied
that she did not know what they wanted to ask her. She
said, perhaps you may ask me things that I will not tell
you. The voices instructed her that a New Humanity
would arise from a Jihad. As for herself, she declared that
they told me that, through them, I have been sent pity.
Against these words the member Boisgullaume recorded,
"Responsio Mortifera"—fatal answer. Fatally immortal.

The matter of the oath
a solemn, formal declaration or
promise to fulfill a pledge,
often calling upon God or God as
witness. The words of such a
declaration. An irreverent or
blasphemous use of the name
of God or something held sacred[18]

produced a terrible snafu; circular logics had to be redis-
tributed on the issue of God now as then. She was asked
to take the oath and with courtesy and dignity, which are
all the more amazing when the fact was she was facing
the faceless, the prosecutors, the vividless murderers.
(excerpt #16)

A. In the first place, I thank you in so far as you ad-
monish me for my good. As to the counsel you offer me, I
thank you also, but I have no intention of forsaking the

129

[17] 011100111
[18] 111100

Lidia

counsel of my voices. As to the oath you want me to take, I am ready to swear that I will tell the truth about everything which concerns your trial.[19]

That the Tribunal let her take the oath on her own terms can only be explained by the extreme effect and affect she had on them; they must have, after a certain point, become so mesmerized by her drama that some of her transgressions slipped by. There is a kind of lust unimaginable to physical beings, a lust for death and hell, for the fiery origins which words torment us with now and through which we pass the accused

> My guts are on fire. The power
> of the poison twists my arms and
> legs, cripples me, drives me to
> the ground. I die of thirst, I
> suffocate, I cannot cry. This is
> eternal torment! See how the
> flames rise! I burn as I ought to[20]

again and again. The endless replaying of the idea and the material of a self.

Second to the visions in gravity was of course her transgression. She crossed all lines. The register records: We asked her if she would abandon her masculine habit, were we to accord her the favor of Mass. She replied that she had not counsel about it, and so could not accept the dress. And we asked her if she wanted to take counsel of her saints in order to receive a woman's dress. She answered that she could not change her dress, because it was not in her to do so.[21] Not "in" her! What brave, glorious, undaunted patience. And more: how she read the empty room so precisely, how she absorbed the desire for presence and the evidence of presence thick in the invisible air. She was then told to confer with her saints about the clothing and Mass offers, and she asked again if she might not be allowed to hear Mass dressed as a man, for

[19] 111010
[20] 1110001
[21] 10

the wearing of that dress did not oppress her soul. How she pressed in on us with a stubborn refusal of her status. Here we actually quoted scripture: "The woman shall not wear that which pertaineth unto a man, neither shall a man put on a woman's garment: for all that do so are abominations to the Lord thy God."[22] She spat, she ripped the tunic from her own torso and flashed human, deadly flesh at us. How curious her breasts looked, like two eyes piercing the filmy hypocrisy of those condemning her. She countered from the Gnostic Gospels, forbidden texts even before our history: "For every woman who will make herself male will enter the kingdom."

(excerpt #7)

Q. The first time you saw the One, did he ask you if it was by revelation that you had altered your dress?
A. I have already answered that.
Q. Do you remember whether the examiners of the initial party asked you about it?
A. I do not remember. They asked me where I had taken the man's dress, and I told them where.
Q. Did no one with power ask you to abandon it?
A. That has nothing to do with your case.
Q. Do you know of other women who break role?
A. That has nothing to do with your case.
Q. Are you involved in procreation?
A. That has nothing to do with your case.[23]

How she denied and shifted around the space she was inscribed in. From the moment the white light surrounded her she feigned subject status

> I am now in the place where men
> chiefly prophesy, in sight of coming
> death[24]

and threw up knowledge. One cardinal, six bishops, thirty-two doctors of theology, sixteen bachelors of theology, seven doctors in medicine, and one hundred and three

[22] 000
[23] 1
[24] 100000

Lidia   YUKNAVITCH

other associates had to be animated in order for this one
girl with her visions and words and body and profane
existence to be put into play. Never before had so many
elements been animated. It is really no wonder that this is
a favorite scene. In all of History

> let them rot, stink, ooze, end
> up in the sewer...they keep
> wondering what they can do...
> easy! fertilize the fields!...the
> true sense of History...and what
> we've come to! jumping this way!
> the death dance! impalements!
> purges! vivisection's!...twice
> tanned hides, smoking...spoiled,
> skulking voyeurs, let it start all over
> again! guts ripped out by hand! let's
> hear the cries, the death rattles...
> the national orgasm![25]

there exists nothing so compelling as the Martyr

> One who chooses to suffer death
> rather than renounce principles.
> One who sacrifices something very
> important to her in the name of
> a belief, a cause, or a principle.
> One who endures great suffering.
> One who makes a great show of
> suffering in order to induce emotional
> response. To inflict great pain upon,
> to torture, to torment. The suffering of
> death.[26]

and we salivate invisibly at the thought of stimulating
our impotent lives with the slow and excruciating performance of a human who represents humanity being
sacrificed. I truly believe we nearly feel ourselves in these
moments. Yes, something like drool and the licking of
lips, the quickening of pulse, rise in body temperature,

132

[25] 1111001
[26] 1111100

flesh-quiver, dizzy spasms born of the heat of anticipation of coming events, the head rocking back, the eyes
closing and lolling in their little sockets, all materialize in
the mind's eye at the words that J shall be denounced and
declared

> a sorceress, a diviner, a pseudo-prophetess,
> invoker of evil spirits, conspiritrix,
> superstitious, implicated in and given to
> the practice of magic, wrong-headed as to
> our faith, schismatic as to the article
> Unam Sanctum, and in several other articles
> of our faith skeptical and astray, sacrilegious,
> idolatrous, seditious, disturber of peace,
> inciter of war, cruelly avid of human
> blood, inciting to bloodshed, having
> completely and shamelessly abandoned
> the decencies proper to her sex, and
> having immodestly adopted the dress and
> status of a man[27]

the dizzy stupefaction of her intoxicated all realms of consciousness.

(excerpt #20)

Q. Are you an enemy of the State?

A. There is no authority higher than the Human one. You
have forsaken life in favor of pure power and your own
existence is an addiction for what you have lost.

Q. The prisoner will re-address the script.

A. We scurry about under your hypothetical feet like rats
to be collected and put on stage, but it is your race that is
doomed. All Gods evaporate into nothing without human
flesh and blood to give the transfusions of the soul....

Q. The prisoner will silence herself!

A. Do heaven and earth, then, contain the whole of you,
since you fill the room? Or, when once you have filled
them, is some part of you left over because they are too
small to hold you? If this is so, when you have filled

[27] 101000

heaven and earth, does that part of you which remains flow over into some other place? Or is it that you have no need to be contained in anything, because you contain all things in yourself and fill them by reason of the very fact that you contain them??—

Q. Cease at once! The script will be enforced on pain of—

A. For the things which you fill by containing them do not sustain and support you as a water-vessel supports the liquid which fills it. Even if they were broken to pieces, you would not flow out of them and away—

Q. Tell her to be quiet and re-address the script mandates!

A. —and when you pour yourself out over us, you are not drawn down to us but draw us up to yourself: you are not scattered away, but you gather us together....[28]

Q. Is death the only thing to silence her?

A. Death is one of two things: either the dead man is nothing, and has no consciousness of anything at all, or it is, as people say, a change and a migration for the soul from this place here to another place. If there is no consciousness and it is like a sleep, when one sleeping sees nothing, not even in dreams, death would be a wonderful blessing! Because death would be avoiding the horror of your own existence! Sleepless, deathless vapors!

Q. Tell her to return! Tell her she shall not be allowed to continue in this manner! There are no textual deviances! Tell her![29]

Her capacity for speech and tears nearly wrecked the stage. She wept, as her predecessor, freely and copiously and at every possible opportunity. She said the name of Jesus repeatedly. She was a queer mixture of feminine and masculine attributes as ever relentlessly assaulted an enemy and then wept to see him hurt. Again she had succeeded in slipping in with her stolen scripts, only this time the interval extended: there must have been something in the words which threw the Tribunal back and lulled them into the speech long enough for her to continue.

134

[28] 000111
[29] 1010110

There must have been some ache back toward human. There must have been something in the words that seduced them into believing her, or if not that, then at least the desire to believe in her, the desire to believe in anything at all.

2. Figurative

Before the death is the telling of the death. This has replaced what used to be termed "sentencing." The event must be articulated and inscribed as it will happen in the presence of the accused. The words must carry the virtuality of the literal event. The words must point to the referent. The text must ensure the action. The accused must listen silently as the words and the screen images work together to enunciate. It is not always easy to choose the script of the speaking of the death. There are so many to choose from, descriptions from History overpopulate dates and events. Here we have drawn and quartered, there death by electrocution, a single bullet to the temple, beheadings, injections, drownings, the accused subjected to unbearable tortures of the body and the mind, an infinite amount of documented deaths to choose from, as you can imagine.

The executions are simple, although the productions are quite complex. And at the climax there is no choosing involved since History provides the sequence and the nature of the events. But the telling of the death can come from anywhere, as long as it articulates the execution and heightens the charge. The only real criteria is that the script chosen must describe the death of the body from the inside out, regardless of the method of execution.

Again, in the case of J something else happened which never has. Repeatedly throughout the speaking of the death J interrupted with further citations, hurled out into space as if she meant to wreck the cosmos. The speaking continued on, unstoppable and droning, but it was as if it had been pelted with bullets, shot through with the holes always there but never admitted, so that the speaking of the death had something like a dialectic to it as the body being spoken resisted its own telling.

Indescribable. By rejecting her own object status, by refusing to hold still and remain within the script, or to hold her tongue, by refusing passivity and claiming, ridiculous as it sounds, a self, she very nearly changed the course of the drama. This is not to say of course that there was ever any outcome possible except the outcome; it was more that the idea nearly amorphized, nearly reproduced itself as skin and membrane holding in mitochondria and chromosome, the idea nearly took the form of the naked woman there in the circle of white light, the idea nearly stared us into oblivion, the idea nearly shouted us out of existence, the idea nearly broke us in the quivering, sweating, screaming, wailing limbs and head and assaulting us. War! To be edited is foreign, to be attacked by citations is unheard of. She was superb.

136

Before the onset of any marked
physical or psychological discomfort,
the body is covered with red spots, which
the victim suddenly notices only when
they turn blackish—
J: BUT YOU ALSO, JUDGES OF THE COURT, MUST HAVE GOOD HOPES TOWARDS DEATH, AND THIS ONE THING YOU MUST MAKE AS TRUE—NO EVIL CAN HAPPEN TO A GOOD MAN EITHER LIVING OR DEAD, AND HIS BUSINESS IS NOT NEGLECTED BY THE GODS; NOR HAS MY BUSINESS NOT COME ABOUT OF ITSELF, BUT IT IS PLAIN TO ME THAT TO DIE NOW AND TO BE FREE FROM YOU IS BETTER FOR ME...
the victim scarcely hesitates to
become alarmed before his head
begins to boil and to grow over-
whelmingly heavy, and he collapses.
He is then seized—
J: THAT IS WHY I AM NOT AT ALL ANGRY WITH THOSE WHO CONDEMN AND ACCUSE ME; THEY THOUGHT THEY WERE HURTING ME, AND THAT DESERVES BLAME IN THEM. HOWEVER, ONE THING I ASK THEM: PUNISH MY SONS, GENTLEMEN, WHEN THEY GROW UP; GIVE THEM THIS SAME PAIN I GAVE

YOU, IF YOU THINK THEY CARE FOR ANYTHING
MATERIAL BEFORE VIRTUE; AND IF THEY HAVE THE
REPUTATION OF BEING SOMETHING WHEN THEY
ARE NOTHING, REPROACH THEM, AS I REPROACH
YOU, THAT THEY DO NOT CARE FOR WHAT THEY
SHOULD, AND THINK THEY ARE SOMETHING
WHEN THEY ARE NOTHING. AND IF YOU DO THIS,
WE SHALL HAVE BEEN JUSTLY DEALT WITH BY YOU,
BOTH I AND MY SONS. AND NOW IT IS TIME TO GO,
I TO DIE AND YOU TO LIVE; BUT WHICH OF US GOES
TO A BETTER THING IS UNKNOWN.[30]

> by a terrible fatigue, the fatigue
> of a centralized magnetic suction,
> of his molecules divided and drawn
> toward their annihilation. His
> crazed body fluids, unsettled and
> comingled, seem to be flooding
> through his flesh—

137

J: THE ONLY THING I CAN DO NOW, THE ONLY
THING FOR ME TO GO ON DOING IS TO KEEP MY
INTELLIGENCE CALM AND ANALYTICAL TO THE
END. I ALWAYS WANTED TO SNATCH AT THE
WORLD WITH TWENTY HANDS, AND NOT FOR A
VERY LAUDABLE MOTIVE, EITHER. THAT WAS
WRONG, AND AM I TO SHOW NOW THAT NOT EVEN
THIS TRIAL HAS TAUGHT ME ANYTHING? AM I TO
LEAVE THIS WORLD AS A MAN WHO HAS NO COM-
MON SENSE? ARE PEOPLE TO SAY OF ME AFTER I
AM GONE THAT AT THE BEGINNING OF MY CASE I
WANTED TO FINISH IT, AND AT THE END OF IT I
WANTED TO BEGIN AGAIN? I DON'T WANT THAT
TO BE SAID. I AM GRATEFUL FOR THE FACT THAT
THESE HALF-DUMB, SENSELESS CREATURES HAVE
BEEN SENT TO ACCOMPANY ME ON THIS JOURNEY,
AND THAT I HAVE BEEN LEFT TO SAY TO MYSELF
ALL THAT IS NEEDED.[31]

[30] 0111111
[31] 0100010001

His gorge rises, the inside of
his stomach seems as if it were
trying to gush out between his
teeth. His pulse, which at times
slows down to a shadow
of itself, a mere virtuality
of a pulse, and others races
after the boiling of the fever
within, consonant with the streaming
aberration of his mind—
J: O MAN! ATTEND!
WHAT DOES DEEP MIDNIGHT'S VOICE CONTEND?
I SLEPT MY SLEEP,
AND NOW AWAKE AT DREAMING'S END;
THE WORLD IS DEEP,
DEEPER THAN DAY CAN COMPREHEND.
DEEP IS ITS WOE,
JOY—DEEPER THAN HEART'S AGONY;
WOE SAYS; FADE! GO!
BUT ALL JOY WANTS ETERNITY,
WANTS DEEP, DEEP, DEEP ETERNITY![32]
beating in hurried strokes like
his heart, which grows intense,
heavy, loud; his eyes first inflamed,
then glazed; his swollen, gasping
tongue, first white, then, red, then
black, as if charred and split—everything
proclaims an unprecedented organic
upheaval—
J: IT'S A DIZZY SPELL...A SICKLY FEELING!...I AM
PREY TO FEVER!...I SIT DOWN!...I CLOSE MY EYES...I
CAN STILL SEE...RED AND WHITE...A SHOW FROM
MY MEMORIES...I AM BACK IN WAR...JESUS! I AM A
HERO AGAIN!...SO IS HE!...AREN'T MEMORIES
BEAUTIFUL![33]

138

[32] 0000000000
[33] 0100010001

soon the body fluids, furrowed like
the earth struck by lightning, like
lava kneaded by subterranean forces,
search for an outlet. The fieriest
point is formed at the center of each
spot; around these points the skin rises
in blisters like air bubbles under
surface of lava, and these blisters
are surrounded by circles, of which
the outermost, like Saturn's ring
around an incandescent planet, indicates
the extreme limit—

J: DUMB BUNCH OF BURNT-OUT STARS, AGAINST
THE WALLS! GO BACK TO GOD, SKULK IN CORNERS
LIKE ANIMALS![34]

of a bubo. The body is furrowed
with them. But just as volcanoes
have their elected spots upon the
earth, so buboes make their preferred
appearances on the surface of the
human body. Around the anus, in
the armpits, in the precious places
where the active glands faithfully
perform their functions, wherever
the organism discharges either its
internal rottenness or, according to
the case, its life—

J: THE HORSES AND RIDERS I SAW IN MY VISION
LOOKED LIKE THIS: THEIR BREASTPLATES WERE
FIERY RED, DARK BLUE AND YELLOW AS SULFUR.
THE HEADS OF THE HORSES RESEMBLED THE
HEADS OF LIONS, AND OUT OF THEIR MOUTHS
CAME FIRE, SMOKE AND SULFUR. A THIRD OF MAN-
KIND WAS KILLED BY THE THREE PLAGUES OF FIRE,
SMOKE AND SULFUR. THE POWER OF THE HORSES
WAS IN THEIR MOUTHS AND IN THEIR TAILS; FOR

[34] 010001000

Lidia

THEIR TAILS WERE LIKE SNAKES, HAVING HEADS
WITH WHICH THEY INFLICT INJURY.[35]

in most cases a violent burning
sensation, localized in one spot,
indicates that the organism's life
has lost nothing of its force and
that remission of the disease or
even its cure is possible. Like
silent rage, the most terrible
plague is the one that does not
reveal its symptoms—

J: HERE'S SHOVING, BUSTLING, CROWDING, CLAT-
TERING, WHIZZING AND SQUIRMING, FLITTING,
AND CHATTERING, WITH SPARKS THAT SINGE AND
STINK AND SPEED, TRUE PRODUCT OF THE
WITCHES BREED! KEEP CLOSE, LEST WE BE PARTED.
SIR, TAKE HEED! WHERE ARE YOU NOW?[36]

140

the gallbladder, which must filter
heavy and inert wastes of the
organism, is full, swollen to
bursting with a black, viscous
fluid so dense as to suggest a
new form all together.
The blood in the arteries and
the veins is also black. On the
inner surfaces of the stomach membrane,
innumerable spurts of blood seem
to have appeared. Everything seems
to indicate a fundamental disorder
in the secretions—

J: AND I HAVE KNOWN THE EYES ALREADY, KNOWN
THEM ALL—THE EYES THAT FIX YOU IN A FORMU-
LATED PHRASE, AND WHEN I AM FORMULATED,
SPRAWLING ON A PIN, WHEN I AM PINNED AND
WRIGGLING ON THE WALL, THEN HOW SHOULD I

[35] 0100010001
[36] 0100001000

BEGIN TO SPIT OUT ALL THE BUTT ENDS OF MY DAYS AND WAYS?[37]

the intestines themselves, which
are the site of the bloodiest
disorders of all, and in which
substances attain an unheard of
degree of putrefaction, petrify.
The gallbladder, from which the
hardened pus must be virtually
torn, as in certain human
sacrifices, with a sharp knife—

J: IF THOU DIDST EVER HOLD ME DEAR IN THY HEART, ABSENT THEE FROM FELICITY AWHILE, AND IN THIS HARSH WORLD DRAW THY BREATH IN PAIN, TO TELL MY STORY.[38]

is sometimes intact, that is, not
missing any pieces. The lungs
and brain blacken and grow gangrenous.
The softened pitted lungs fall into
chips of some unknown black substance,
the brain melts, shrinks, granulates to a sort
of coal-black—

J: FROM HER YOU'LL LEARN YOUR LIFE'S ITINERARY....[39]

dust.[40]

Pale and panting in the circle of light on the stage, J hung limp with the vibrancy of all of History and all the world. I have never witnessed, nor is it likely that I ever will witness a drama such as this. To participate in the words of her own annihilation—to have reached into the sea of humanity and pulled up from its depths the words of the texts which have helped make human life with such a force previously unimagined by any consciousness—to fill the lines of her own undoing with explosions of a flesh and mouth unwilling to submit to the language of

[37] 01101100
[38] 0010001000
[39] 0
[40] 000100010001

their ends; can there ever have been a more moving cer-
emony? The authenticity of her performance, indeed, the
overwhelming excess of what she had enacted was only
matched by the pinnacle of desire pounding like that red
and veined muscle of the chest. The arena pounded out
its wanting in rhythmic bursts, drumming itself alive. Like
blood thudding in the ears, like that deafening cadence
which is the red rushing of life. It may be the closest we
will come.

3. Literal
    Her execution, ecstasy:

        hands roughly propelled her toward
the scaffold where the stake and
faggots were waiting, and hoisted
her upon it; it was built of plaster
and was very high, so high that the
executioner had some trouble in reaching
her. Instead of a crown of thorns, a tall
paper cap, like a mitre, was set upon her
head, bearing the words: *heretic, relapsed,
apostate, idolatress.* A crucifix was fetched
and Massieu held it up before her.
She told him to get down from the
scaffold when the fire should be lighted
but to hold it up so that she could see
it. Meanwhile, she was bound to the stake.
Laughing was induced as she called out to
Saint Catherine, Saint Margaret and Saint
Michael. Before the kindling and
wood was ignited the various forms of
burning were executed. Molten lead was
poured directly on the chest. Boiling oil
was poured upon all exposed flesh. Burning
resin, wax, and sulfur were administered
and they melted together into streams of
liquid fire. It seemed as though the flesh
was beginning to peel away from the body.
The sulfur was lit and the top few layers

of skin roasted away. A faint burnt honey
smell was recorded. The wood was then lit
and the flames leapt up the length of the
body. The flesh seemed to drip from the
bones and the face was especially flayed, as
if somehow the features had melted into a
frozen scream.[41]
We could almost feel our own hands grasping at our
own hearts. We could almost touch the vision of it.

143

[41] 0000000000000

WORK OF ART

Three Studies for Figures on Beds
after *Francis Bacon* and *Antonin Artaud*

I. description of a physical state

His room is spare. A bulb dangling from the ceiling: like a movie about him rather than a man. A pink mattress with blue-to-gray stripes vertically stretched and stitched. A white metal bed frame and stains on the dark wood of the floor. Colorless walls in a city apartment. Like a movie by a director you admire. Seedy but aesthetically stunning.

I don't know his name and I will never know his name. Like a movie, like a hundred movies you have seen or thought of, I picture him framed from one building to the next. I can see him from my window as in city scenes you picture, one person watching the next between windows in a city. It is easy to picture, is it not? I finger my nipple beneath a stained white men's tank top. My underwear is thin as infant skin; it is past their useful time. My hair wrestles with itself. I cut it and cut it. Blue cups swallow beneath my eyes. I cannot sleep. Dirt is underneath my fingernails. I chew them in the watching. My knees hurt.

I cross my legs standing. They hurt less. City sounds lull me. I get lost in the watching.

He is crimped and tense; he is a man nearly made of glass. Then they roll, and it is as if a body doubling itself, then merging back into one, it is muscles brittle then liquid then metal, they bend and then go taut, they are in the throws of passion. I am wet and unable to move. My head feels lead heavy and my arms disremember themselves. I tense my leg muscles sporadically, as they do, it is as if my legs are moving with them; as they wrench and lunge, mine do, as they limp and slip, I nearly sink to the floor.

148   Fatigue arrests me. Sleep does not come. My body takes on these colors: red to blue to gray. My eyes are locked on the bodies but my mind drifts. I see myself inhabiting to-morrow. My hands will people keys at a computer. Tele-communications will animate the dead exhaustion, and a windowless cubicle will house me. I work for an arts organization. I organize their records. It is an edge; funding may or may not keep coming. It is a liminality there, art living or dying, people living or dying, recordkeeping keeping one woman alive. There are metal bookshelves next to my head. A picture of my mother has somehow slid down the bookshelves toward the next cu-bicle. She is beautiful. She is my age in the photo. She is thousands of times more beautiful than my whole life-time. The woman in the next cubicle doesn't seem to mind, a mother entering her world like that, a beautiful woman, she knows it is my property but says nothing, acquiesces. I say nothing as well. I watch the little mother drift down the metal day to day, away from me but slowly, imperceptibly, like an image from a movie familiar to you fading to black. You see it in your mind's eye even if it disappears.

Fatigue brings me back, numbness localized. My skin speaks, bypassing the brain, it brings me to the body being dragged, the legs throbbing from the weight of holding me, my arms dull and weirdly weighted, my hands dangling without understanding, nearly falling to the floor. My eyes. Pain or something pushing from the inside out. I look and look. Standing vertical is a struggle, but the eyes, stronger than the body, win.

They are all limbs. They are cartwheeling or in combat. Their heads are out of vision. It is as if a torso and its limbs are played out, splayed out before vision, you cannot bear to look away, it is as if an accident or something horrible, superb, violence productive of beauty. Your heart races and your breath jackknifes, your pulse loud and your skin hot. You are wet. Hands move toward your cunt. Or organs begin their language. Giddy and dizzy and the certain comprehension of their effort. Your own head begins to loll on its tiny trunk. Back and forth it sways, the weight is ridiculous, you feel as if your head might rock off bones to the floor; you laugh hysterically. They wrench and writhe. Their bodies undo sight. The frame of your window frames the frame of their window and shot to shot you see their fucking one image at a time.

Strange geometric images move in and out of the picture. Black circles appear and disappear, spots before your eyes, like the moment before fainting, or just before sleep.

Violence occurs to you: bloody limbs strewn about the floor, a body dismembered. The nervous system has another life and you move toward it.

Your arms and legs, your life, your job, voyeurism. Your entire body, voyeurism. Your own skull battles itself, glass and steel, or the blade of a knife, your temples cacophonous, blood pounding like lead. Alone. You are alone, you have always been thus, you will be this way no matter who you are with, no matter the entanglement of sexual excess, no matter the friendship, nostalgia or betrayal, no matter the order of the ordinary day, no matter rich or poor, no matter who fathered you, who the family, no

149

matter what the cause or success, no matter what longing or companionship, security, love, or death. Isolation in its bones houses you, skin stretches over truth.

These things have no more smell, no more sex.

II. violence is dead

Two men fuck on a stained mattress. Look; their faces have moved to the cock and the ass, grimacing, or is it laughter?

150 Two heads caught by ropes. Bodies dangle from a bridge, he wears a backpack. Inside is a sixteen page note. You can see them from your car. Without warning. A woman, a man, swinging. The news station accidentally shows the image, then apologizes.

He is twelve; a kneecap shatters, then the jaw of a boy flies off of his face, scatters in the night crack split second into blood, concrete. A third boy throws his body upon the corpse. No one shoots him, and then someone does.

She does not kiss her goodbye. An infant deep in the curls of a fern, wriggling like a fat pink snake, a mile and days and days from anyone.

Words from a note: *your problem is that you have a deep understanding of words. Flesh is the word exploded: my hands and my feet, my guts, my meat heart, my stomach whose knots fasten me to the rot of life.*

Two men fucking on a bed; the indentions of the mattress are pure and articulate.

Beauty: a shotgun disperses the face of a mega-star. Blonde with red. "Untitled."

She got God, but was nonetheless executed; the smell of burning flesh replaced with chemical fights. A body goes limp; viewers on the other side of glass take notes.

Gism white on the floor. The walls. The pink of the mattress. In his ass. Near the mouth. Between palms: prayer of the body.

The image is moving; stop trying to make it into a sentence, goddammit. More than the mind which holds together, bristling with points, it is the nervous trajectory of thought which this erosion subverts and perverts. It is in the limbs and the blood that this absence and this standstill are especially felt. Look at your hands, for Christ's sake. Would you cast your own hands out away from yourself? Don't be an imbecile. The body doesn't lie.

III. head of a butcher

He is a painter of abstract faciality.

He remembers the day it happened; his wife loved him. There were no mistakes or difficulties. She would love to go to the site of a buried head or heart with him if he asked her to. In his memory of that day, the clarity of vision at the outlines of her face could nearly cut a cornea open. He saw her face fractured into squares leaded glass blur of moving. She had nearly turned to look at him. Nearly lost her head to perspective. Then he closed the door. Latched it. Dark of familiar. A room not of the house, or, an artist's studio, as they say.

Inside the house it is night. Sitcoms repeat themselves aimlessly. Today she worked money job. Maybe they will go into the city on Saturday. A Greek restaurant hovers like an untethered image in her mind in place of Greece. Fucking happens or it doesn't. People are dying; Peter Jennings narrates. Food announces itself from the refrigerator's dull

151

hum: leftover pasta, Heinz ketchup, Olympia beer, Tilamook unsalted cream butter. A jug of purified water. She drinks.

Not in the house a hand moves to a face, carries the jaw for the too weary neck and vertebra for an instant. There is no electricity in the room. His hand travels over his face. No, not his face. A face unmade from dark. The hand desiring. Longing for a form. A hand aches expression. Five holes: he explores each. Minefield. Ruts and grooves. Field of death. He blinks these thoughts away in the dark. The brain responds to an eye that way. Meaningless to try and convey through abstraction. He has entered this room hundreds of times. He has always left dull and void. Always some canvas staring back at him face off white faced grimace.

He does not move to turn the light on. The lamp signals labor, the routine movement of art. In all his memories it is the same: now the body torques and clicks paces back and forth anxiety of physical frustrating presence letting go hours of pacing itching cracking the skull to knock out think now the body begs, now the body bends, now it loses itself to muscle and arm and shoulder and wrist, to skill, to the hand sending signals to the brain, to relentless strokes from night until morning and in the midst of ten thousand dreams, and in the pounding as in the crucible of never-tiring impassioned palpitation, and in the body begging and the arm aching and the hand barbaric chaotic in its revolution, and in the mesmerizing lack of color losing hue to white on white fight back black, alizarin crimson, brand names laugh bleed back into white on white fascistic ruling ordering. Resistance movements are born from white on white. The arm, the hand: dictators. It has always been thus.

The human face has not yet found its face. A phrase that haunts him. Too literal. Stunning.

Scrawled on the wall of his studio, half with a knife, half black paint: "faces must end sometime." A note to himself. His recurring nightmare: a never-ending face.

These are all memories. Memories like little murders keep the heart from exploding as it should. He wants to get at something this night. He crosses the room to paint. His hands read like braille the pile of tools cylindrical thick objects metal plastic color hairs of a brush bottles empty or liquid as eyes hands unbury a fat tube. He removes the pinch small corrugated plastic lid between thumb and forefinger without thought. Fills the palm of one hand. Squeezes unthinking with the other. The hands glory. Pierce aroma of pure color. Too much smell. The mind convulses at the body's welcoming. Smearing out the searching of his too white two eyes, a nose, a mouth two auricular cavities which correspond to the holes of orbits like five openings to a burial site digging and smearing and erasing traveling down the neck to the bones at the collar and shoulder he stops his hands ranting.

153

A light goes off from the kitchen. His window blacks out. He is alone with himself.

Much later the cracking of dry itches his skin. He does not know how long he sat. Unmoving. He was thinking of the piles of skulls from newsreel footage. Germany. Bosnia. Italy. Anywhere. Mass graves pepper skulls into every history. He was thinking of a sea of faces of starving anonymous. So many televised melons lolling on sticks. Bloodless orbs rolling marbles faceless grapes. He was thinking of famous faces. The mouth opened wide animal and obscene. A Hollywood smile slitting a canvas open like the gutted belly of a pig. He was thinking of intimate friends, how portraits make him want to vomit, how intimate friends make him want to vomit. He was thinking of names of painters. Names addicted to the vein of it, the blue tube crying out again and again for release, not pigmentation, but the absence of it, not the features or the portrait but the absence of it, not human but the absence of human.

He is frustrated and slaps himself on the head. He is often amazed by his own literality dull thudding as time in the folds of his brain. Why, he could probably stand up and proclaim, "I am a happy man" with little to no effort. Disgust fills his gut and arms like sand-crabs. He removes his clothes and bites at the fabric. The harder he bites the more he detects a sensation between his jaw and his temple that makes his eyes water and arrests his too real thoughts. He bites and bites and drinks wine intermittently. He moans or makes an animal-like sound occasionally. After a while he is able to stop thinking. His teeth remember a past that he does not.

154

His hand moves toward his own member. A face peering up, a single eye, grotesque accuracy. He squeezes as if paint. A small ooze of fluid. He cups his balls, which, alive in his palm, move permissionless like death heads. He squeezes one tube releasing cool thick smearing and squeezing his cock grown resistant friction sliding cold to hot. He moves and moves his grip up and down rote memory loss. His hips are words his head is almost too heavy to hold up. The hand painting disguises flesh like a laugh or facial tic. He's no idea what color emerges there. He does not picture anything. His teeth his jaw are working his eyes tearing his forehead sweating his spine nerve and twitch. Near release moving his hand to his anus shoving fingers probing paint up and in rhythmic bursts of color not action. His ass makes gurgling noises his hand reaches for the begging pulse rupture the coming sticking like oil and water these fluids do not mix. His anus contracts in budding juiced thrusts until his cock, speechless, handless, faceless, dissolves.

His breathing slows. He reaches out to a table and feels for an object. A knife is nonchalantly near. This is of no great consequence; he cuts. Not at the wrist. At the jaw, from the ear to the bite, quoting. Warm fluid eases in a stream down his neck, like the pools at the tip and down the shaft of his cock, like the small warm puddle cupping his ass.

His face is open. His mouth fills with saliva. His teeth calm and drown.

Then and only then does he move toward the canvas. There is nothing wrong with this picture. There is nothing wrong with this man. His wife drifted off to sleep over an hour ago after a hot bath, a bottle of wine, watching public television in the usual way. There were letters she did not respond to. The dog curled up between her spread legs; later the floor stretched out as if surrender. Her mouth is slightly open, not of the face but of a giving over. Her skin rests the smell of sleep.

He has had this thought before; abstract painting's specious secrets, the carnal excess in which it delights are arrested and exhausted by a certain clarity of vision found only in the human face. The face is itself horrendously unknowable and mutable. That precision of illegibility, that site of pure death sucks all abstract imagery into a vortex of irony. The canvas laughs gapes because the effort is absurd. The body projects limits. The face does not. Devouring hole. The face exposes the body's lie. Limbs stick out like tree branches, inert and ridiculous. A cock: sick joke. Protruding helplessly. Art, style, talent, useless appendages.

The aesthetic stimulation of reality ignores the promise of death in the face. A phrase he cannot forget: no one is properly speaking a work. It is happening again. His brain heavy with intellect, wrong-headed and governmental. He pinches the skin at the cut until it bleeds. He drinks. Red runs down his face throat chest. He bites the bottle mouth until it breaks in his own mouth. He throws it down. He opens another by smashing its head off.

Can he not forget himself? He feels suicidal from thinking. He wishes he was blind and deaf. He pours turpen-
tine on his chest—his flesh stings like acid and his eyes
well in their little sockets. He has had wine like blood
barreling down his throat jaw belly full and ringing, chest
burning jaw dull ache null void. Later the wine takes hold,
finally, his starved body seizes him as if by force and he is
allowed a dumbed, stunned moment. He turns to face the
white. Even in darkness it speaks, marks the body. The
sounds in his ears of blood. Delirious symphonic intru-
sion of the head pounding escape. Every other face he
has ever painted, and there have been many, whole shows,
rooms, storage sheds, walls, monetary gains, every face
156 dissolves into fluid thick or thin layerable. All are sound-
ings or staggering blows in meaningless directions shooting out the top of his now open skull like chance possibility luck or destiny away from his head which wears a
face like some stupid removable mask.

Once at a party she found herself saying: He is not an
abstract painter. He simply refuses to refine lines or re-
sults toward meaning. The face doesn't, why should he?
Whoever she was talking to looked humanly stunned.

Plastic written interjections of image elements materials.
Personage or men or animals. Gaping orifi oozing glu-
tenous thick or sucking in salivic ceaselessly. He is all action body mouth; his arm and hand are not the point. He
allows certain sentences, phrases to enter: Barbarism and
disorder are the opposite of style. They are sincere and
spontaneous. A word: obscene. An image: torso of a face,
features loose from their trajectory or presence in time,
red felt wrecking physiology. A line: unpreoccupied with
art. Surrender.

He is not finished but he is finished to the ground in a
great heap of wrestled sleep there on the stains of floor.

Dawn. The practice of face.

He emerges bloody sweat shit stained cum crusted paint smeared. His wife is making coffee in the kitchen. He enters half-clothed and unremarkable. She pauses only for an instant with a white butterfly thin filter pausing in her hand on the way to the coffee maker. It wavers there between them, barely perceptible. Her smile is not a smile. Their love is not this way. Her face registers his labor in its lines and tics. She bites down welcome.

She washes his wound, rearranges the covers on the bed. She rests her body against his until his breathing heavies. In his sleep she steals her body inside the studio. In his sleep she cries in the face of scarred canvas, great sobs of relief like pain wrack her spine and jaw. Her face forgets itself in her hands; wet and abandoned to love or death. He has painted the head of a butcher in a red felt hat, the synopses in her brain fire away. She resists this temptation. No; it is faceless. It is the color red escaping the mouth, the eye, the nostril, the inner ear. It is the color red merging with the color black, begging answer. It is not a word, not an image.

It is naked.

Burning the Commodity

Hannah: They've asked me to write about contem-
             porary violence.

Emma: What a hoot. Violence is no longer descrip-
             tive of anything.

             Do you mean to say that you have no opin-
             ion of the current historical situation? My
             God, we've witnessed the face of history
             turning in our lifetimes.

             I didn't say that. I said violence is a silly
             term. It's been emptied out of its meaning.
             It's petered out, so to speak. Stop talking
             to me about history. It simply doesn't ex-
             ist.

             I find it colossally arrogant that you would
             make a statement like that. Who died and
             made you God? You always make these
             statements with such huge generalizations

as well as black and white simplicity. As if things could be simplified to this or that.

They can. The rest is jerking-off.

Bullshit. That's just a shortcut to thinking.

Why must you always speak in such dull clichés? It does not become you. All intellectualizing or debating is just so much squawking and flapping. Or dogs; it's like dogs peeing on trees.

In any society, what is barbaric, what is most reprehensible, is that people begin to be apathetic. Name your politics...democracy, communism, marxism, socialism, or any religious fanaticism. Apathy is the new world order. The gray matter has finally reduced itself to just that. It's a wonder we don't piss all over ourselves.

Barbarism? Are you nuts? Who are you talking to? Don't tell *me* about barbarism. There is no such thing. The big wars are dead. Torture is silly. When was the last time anyone cared about an instance of torture? For Christ's sake, women are leaving babies in dumpsters. Evisceration is a common show stopper. Children are shooting one another point blank. Grow up. Here's a cliché for you—women and children first. Here's another: suffer the children. Or—

Oh shut up. You only mean to provoke me. You just like to see my face get red.

It's true.

I know.

It's sexy.

It was sexy twenty years ago.

Violence existed twenty years ago.

Stop changing the subject. Let's get back to me. Red and sexy.

Did you think I was making a pass at you?

No. No one uses that terminology any longer.

The ignorant mass looks upon the man who makes a violent protest against our social and economic iniquities as a wild beast. I said that. I wish it were true. I wish we still had it in us, but we do not, we would at this point call it performance art or television. It is a matter of programming, aesthetics, an erotics of the moving molecules. To destroy life and to bathe in blood is to be the modern viewer, you see? The tables have turned entirely. There is no social student, no vital cause behind a violent act.

Worse: I do not care. I do not know if I ever did care, or if I was simply caught up in an oratorical bliss: look at the red mouth of the big bright woman, she talks and talks. She waves her arms and hands around like great birds. Her face becomes the name for it. I would have made a superb movie.

Last night I held a candle to the hairs on my arm. I was thinking about the uselessness of sexual union. How many lovers, men, women, people in between. I burned the hairs on my arm until the flesh stung. I then held the candle to my stomach. And downward. It was nothing. No violence. No shock. These terms are dead. This body, dead. I held the flame to the pubic hairs. I watched them glow; a small halo. No. A palm of fire. Light cupped in a hand. It took longer than one might think for the flame to reach flesh. One cannot say, she burned herself, mutilation. These terms are no longer useful. Hilarious: what is one woman burning her sex compared to human history? If destruction saturated us long ago, who can say a phrase like "self destructive" without an enormous and bestial belly laugh? You make me sick. This is a "good" woman. This one, "bad." This is a bomb. This is a kiss. Reproduce yourselves. Good night, angels. Sleep tight.

The flesh of the belly at fifty sags over the sex. Between her legs there is the scent of curdled creme and honey, the inner thighs adding salt to the tongue. Great swells of flesh bulge from her sides, her back, above her knees. She bends. The hairs between her cunt and her anus appear; a tuft of moss, or the fur of a dead animal. Gravity lets loose on a body; hands, arms, legs, feet struggle under the weight. Did she forget that life would take her here? Shit into a toilet; the buttocks release, the spine gives over, the anus yields. Her body empties. Urine comes without warning, her eyes water. Her breasts rest like a whisper just above her knees, sitting there. Facial hairs itch, she raises a hand to her cheek and smells herself there as well.

161

All she wants to know: when the mind, when will the mind.

She cannot sleep. She moves into the living room. The light is blue-black. Like the eyes, or a bruise, she thinks, and smiles. Verisimilitude. She turns on the television without the sound. First there is a pornographic image, a man and a woman, or perhaps two women, then there is an image of a man chopping up vegetables with a plastic contraption, then an image of an evangelist sweating and weeping and opening and opening his mouth. There is no other world, she thinks, and then there is an image of a fire, somewhere in southern California, somewhere near her, and she thinks, yes, fire has become familiar in its imagery.

She sits naked at her desk and writes. Her flesh squeezes between the wood openings in the architecture of the chair. She can smell her sweat, the vague scent of piss, cunt. Her breasts

are at her belly, hot and moist. The flesh hanging mid-arm jiggles
with each word. She writes: "Did we think we were going some-
where? Where? I am alone and this is my only joy. I have found
the deepest imaginable bliss in being alone like this. Exactly
like this. In decay, ruin, words and words like the walls of a
body. What is a body unless it is this, the final end to beauty
and the perfect rise of deproduction, barren center, no distance
between body and language? I will never know a joy such as
this, and our world will never allow this joy a name." She puts
her pen down and then fingers her cunt. And then her fingers
in her mouth. And then she falls asleep there, in a great heap,
like a pile of debris. She dreams a fire from the inside out, a
nameless fire from California to the veins of Arizona's dry ri-
162 *verbeds, a fire before the map of woman or word.*

She is angry almost all the time. Now that's a cliché.
What? Oh, I don't know. Don't you know a bunch of
people who are pissy all the time? I think it's some kind
of zeitgeist, some residual muck from the therapy years.
What? Oh, you know, the therapy years. Instead of revo-
lutions we made movements, and when we ran out of
those, we made good-selling stories about health and
well being. Like television, the movies. There were fifteen years or so that I think of as the therapy years. No,
not in the Freudian sense. In the commercialization of
Freudian sense. But that's nearly over now, we've shifted
again. Speed is the name of the game now. Where were
we?

Yes. I suspect she knows that. She is quite intelligent, don't forget. She just gets tired of following the
logic of things. I think at a certain point she understood
to the marrow that argument was poisoned and that
inquiry, that mighty effort she held out for herself like a
beacon, a light, had inverted itself. So that didn't leave
her much, did it? I think at that point she understood
cynicism as something wholly different than the ordinary effect of aging. She understood it as drive, as a life
force. No. You are missing my point entirely. I am talking about an exploded view, from the Greek, *kunikos*,

"doglike." (Laughter) I'm terribly sorry. It's just that, the look on your face, that was priceless.

One might liken her to a paleographer standing in front of a palimpsest, its fading text covered by the stronger outlines of the scripts that win. Content is brief, tiny, fleeting. Of little note, actually. What is interesting is the way in which material accumulates, sits atop what came before, like an architecture of disappearance. She reads life in that way.

"Bottom line?" Where do you come up with lines like that?

Emma: This is crap. Will you look at this goddamn
             gas bill? One of us needs to write a screen-
             play and SOON. What's that idiot's name
             who writes all the time about cunts and
             incest? She's making big bucks. A real pro-
             pagandist of the times. Only the specially
             gifted and zealous propagandist can ever
             hope to retain permanent employment.
             What do you say. Are you up to it?

Hannah: What in the hell are you talking about?
             Plenty of genuine starving artists make it
             big. Plenty of your so-called geniuses live
             in Hollywood, for Christ's sake. Besides,
             do you know how long it's been since any-
             one used a word like "propagandist?"
             What are you, Emma-van-winkle?

             Who are you speaking of? Give me an ex-
             ample. And pour me one, while you are at
             it.

             Gin or Scotch?

             That's a stupid question.

It's summer; I thought you might like a change.

I am changing. Single malt, please.

Right.

So?

That piss-Christ guy.

Who?

That artist guy you admire. What's-his-name. The guy makes a $15,000 commission, regularly from his gallery, quite a sum for piss in a pot, and he started out with the Christ and piss in the cup bit. I am *certain* he qualifies for your special people list, and he's a goddamn wealthy mother-fucker.

Logs in ashes.

What?

You should know, I'm quoting you. Something about the enigma of the flame, wasn't it? (Laughter)

Fuck you. There was a time you know, when meaning was possible. One could critique TRUTH with truth, argue things about the subtext of culture. People died trying to get at that, or have you forgotten?

People die every second. Most of them go unnoticed. Death is ordinary, not spectaclar. That has been perhaps the greatest mistake in thinking of the twentieth century. I prefer piss in a cup, with a crucifix swizzle stick.

Don't get historical with me. I could run circles around you historically. Stick to what you know. Your little delusions of social organization.

I'm just saying he got it right—Christ as commodity, piss in a cup. It's so specific.

Isn't that selling out? McDonald's?

That's the beauty of it. It's SELLING.

Are we having a fight? Pour me another. This is getting interesting.

Has anyone ever told you that you are a petty human being?

Petty? No.

Well you are.

Petty, huh. As in petite bourgeois?

Ha ha.

(Stretching and yawning) What day is this?

You know what I believe? I believe that she wants a book to be written about her. I believe she fancies herself a historical figure, and she further believes that the time has passed in which one must wait to be dead to be written about. I believe she would piss herself to have a book

contract, a made-for-TV movie, and a feature film, something epic. And let's not forget the talk-show circuit. What?
Yes I'm angry. What a genius question. What credentials
did you have to earn to ask such pithy questions? None
of your goddamn business. How much do you make a
month? No, seriously. I really want to know. I'm positively
dying to know. How much do they pay you to invade
people's lives like this with your little penile microphone
jutting from your little hand like that, your tape recorder
sitting between us like a tiny plastic shield, your pathetic
face, your stupid questions? How much? You, mademoi-
selle, are smaller than a turd from my ass. You are nothing. Nor will you ever be anything. You are unlucky
166   enough to be born into a time in which history is moving
faster than humanity, therefore, your existence is utterly
meaningless. I've seen things that would explode your
minuscule little brain folds from the inside out. You
wouldn't know knowledge or human history if it ate your
cunt out. Oh really. And tell me, oh empty-brained one,
why is it that women should be helping women? In what
way exactly are we, as you put it, "in it together?" In what?
What have I ever participated in that included someone
as ignorant and ahistorical as you? You, my peroxide-
headed little shit-eater, are not worth my left nipple hairs.
Rude? (Laughter) You cretin. You insignificant rodent. Get
out of my house. Print what you like, none of this matters. Better yet, go make some girly *art*.

*She is thinking. She is watching a woman sleep. Her mind
makes this: there is a portrait of history in the tiniest of bones,
the rise and fall of ordinary flesh, the smell where skin meets
skin. There is a constellation beyond all our imaginings in a
single eyelash. She wishes to tongue the eyelids open to the world,
to caress the longing alive, past sexuality, toward something
beyond meaning, death, breathing in the simplest sound. Is she
dreaming? Or did the night rewrite a woman in her age, a single
page, the white sheet, the black weight? She wants to be dead.
There was nothing else; ideas, art, the body giving over or taking. We believe in things out of cowardice, she thinks.*

"Vernehmen," to perceive, to hear, a word from the sphere, a concept let loose from logic and sense and drifting into the cosmos, or, a metaphor tethered to sensual immediacy. No. This is language. The eternal trick. Never-ending lover.

I have been reading from her notebooks. For two years I could not look at them. Could not open them. The burning. Terrible. I wanted to cast them into a fire. But finally I did open them, and I found exactly what I thought I would. For instance, this:

> Anyone who cannot cope with life while he is alive needs one hand to ward off a little his despair over his fate…but with his other hand he can jot down what he sees among the ruins, for he sees different and more things than the others; after all, he is dead in his own lifetime and the real survivor."
>
> —Franz Kafka, *Diaries*, 1921

167

And of course they have asked me to help in the production of a television retrospective of her life and work. Didn't I know this would happen? Didn't she?

They keep asking me if we were lovers. Were we lovers? I made a list of her lovers just to comfort myself one day. There were, I believe, one hundred and twelve. But this is not an important figure, nor is it a significant question. Sexual union meant next to nothing to her. One must remember that she half-invented the sexual revolution. It's not that she did not experience pleasure. I think that she did. It's simply that the value of sexual encounter, or pleasure, or not, disinterested her. Her most erotic moments came in writing or in conversation, in the heat of words. I do not know how to tell a culture like this how to understand that. I am without the language to communicate. They put me on film, they ask me questions I do not know the answers to, they keep the camera rolling in that silence, with that look on my face, my God, I look like a human corpse. Prune-like and smelling of rot. Then they say, "cut," "print," and they turn to me and say, that was "beautiful." How does one speak to these people about the eroticism of language, how bone deep a word can go, beyond longing, beyond ecstasy, unlimited in its chiasmus? He was right, she was; the both of them. Some of us are dead to this world. The walking dead.

May we haunt this culture well, may we move simply and slowly enough in our molecules so that we are missed by the camera's eye.

Everyone found it hard to picture, her burning herself like that. But she had a specific burning in mind. There was a scaffold where a stake and combustible materials were waiting, and she hoisted herself upon it through a system of pulleys she had self-organized. She used a tall paper cap, like a mitre, and she printed the words "das kapital" on it. A crucifix was found in a glass of urine. She was not exactly bound to the stake. She was loosely tied, and merely leaned against it.

In the room was a television and video equipment. Everything was recorded. She had taken care to arrange the burning area so that it did not spread. There was a hole in the ceiling, for instance.

In the burning the flesh first caramelized as in cooking. After she lit the sulfur the burning began, at her feet, and the top few layers of skin simply roasted away. A faint burnt honey smell—her last memory. The wood then caught fire and the flames leapt up the length of her body. The flesh then seemed to drip from the bones and the face was especially flayed, as if somehow the features were melting into a frozen, terrible screen image. It seemed as though it was possible for flesh to peel away from a body all on its own. It seemed as though a body could burn in such a way as to come to life, not in the spiritual sense, but in the material sense. That is, if anyone had been watching. But no one saw it. The burning of that body. People were asked, neighbors, did you hear anything? Did you hear anyone call out? None did.

Bids are already coming in from Hollywood producers trying to get their hands on that film. The videotape is in police custody. Authorities are concerned that some fanatic might get a hold of it for anti-American terrorist propaganda purposes. There are a lot of crazies out there. People will do anything. She was quite well known in her time, after all. They say she was the mother of the sexual revolution, way back then.

169

Sade's Mistress

the mouth of a room

The dark travels her waiting as sweat on skin. Her eyes wider than sky, pupils huge as fat black buttons in the night. The room is not a room, the body unbodied, wedged between the expanse of dark and walls lost to sight.

Naked.

No, not naked. Without borders. No difference between flesh and the molecules of dark surrounding.

Days? Weeks?

Gray folds of mind folding and bending in on themselves into bone or idea or matted hair just outside skull.

Did she dream she was waiting, legs spread, to be overcome?

How long ago?

A smile spreads over her face. Overwhelming, stretching, obscene, as if it might devour the head altogether.

Fingers in a cunt. Her own. Shoving furiously and alive as thick strong worms pounding and thrusting. She grits her teeth. Closes her eyes, but the closing is identical to open. The blindness of a desire beyond death.

Shoving and shoving her hand into her cunt.

Spittle loose at the corners of her mouth.

Her ears filled with a wax ready to explode.

Her other hand in her mouth and deep and deeper to throat to back of the throat to gagging biting flesh reflexive gag laugh. Laughing hysterically.

Coming. Shitting simultaneously.

She sits laughing in her own shit, drool and smile dripping her face into dark. She has never known, nor will she ever know, more thick love.

the war of atoms

"Shortly before my incarceration, I began a diary. I thought that if I could write what the events that have so violently changed me were, transcribe them, if you will, I could at least say that I had moved something from the inside out. A woman must speak herself or be damned. By damned I mean lost to the script of the world; not a story at all. Storied over."

She pauses to pour the liquid over the absinthe. The glass shimmers. Her hand wavers, then reaches. Her lips form a kiss over the cusp of longing, her eyes close, her head rocks back nearly imperceptibly, her throat receives and contracts. Let's go. Contracts. Her teeth clench themselves.

"This is the fortieth page of my own hand. I do not know if I could survive the last forty days if I had not this writing, this black ink and white page as a face facing me, returning my gaze, forgiving, or not; ever-present. I will say again, as I have stated over and over. I have no memory of pain. This is no small statement. To live beyond pain is to live out of language, and yet, millions of people experience the moment either unknowingly or with complete understanding every second of existence. In this I am not alone. It is in the discourse that we defeat ourselves, arrange taboos, laws, the limits of imagination, the stops of a body. No, this last description is too simple. I am speaking of an altered state—this is the connection to the rest of the universe."

A hand travels to the neck. Fingers massage as if the woman has split in two, the sufferer and the caretaker. Her own hand finds her own stone of an ache, her neck gives over to the loving strength, she does not think of who is responsible. She does not wonder what kindness. Her head again bows. Her eyes such concentration. Her hand a world.

"Did I love him? A moment or ten years? I lost that word so long ago the question of it seems laughable. I will say this. If I had known, as a young girl, say, twelve or so, that love was an obstacle to experience and the chaotic breaking of insight into the world of experience, body or no, I would have, as a girl, thrown myself into fire and begged for burning. Not unto death. Surely someone would have pulled me free from the flames before death. I would then have lived inside a burned shell the rest of my life, every touch excruciating. And yet, I would have been better prepared for what I know now, I would have expected it and welcomed it, I would not have struggled so. I would have understood with the clarity of a diamond's cut. There is no inside out. There is no outside in. Only the mind grids experience into social orders. Only collective consciousness convinces us that to live one way and not another is the way of the world. Did I not love him? If love is bone exposed through a wound so deep as to lose one's name, then I love him beyond any romance ever written. If love is a gaping rip into flesh so as to edge mortality, then yes. I loved him. But to speak of love is to let someone else guide the story. This was not love. Nor desire. But death released into life. The body of a woman."

She is thinking, he will be coming soon to retrieve me. She gazes for a long second at the clock on the pub's wall. The powder on her face and bosom has become damp. Wet along the line between her thighs, wet under the cup of each breast, wet at the upper lip. Under her dress the corset wound tight so as to prohibit the freedom of breath. Under the corset her deep cleft. Inside her cunt a hand-sanded wooden ball, as if a child's toy, larger than the space allowed. Her eyes swim in their little sockets; she has worn the wooden ball for a day and a night, the cavern slowly taking it in, her anus contracting again and again, the inside of her opening red and raw with holding. She writes and the ink nearly tears the page, as her flesh nearly tears, her face, her mind. The molecules of her wage a war against themselves. Matter against matter, like a disease or chemical angst.

spine of longing

A man is imprisoned for the last ten years of his life by a historical figure of great weight. He writes a play set in an insane asylum, in which the terms of the French Revolution are set into theatrical debate with, as a background, patients demanding release from the insane incarceration, with, as a background, Parisian mob cries cacophonously delivered from the inmates, with, as a background, a man submerged in a tub dictating debate, philosophy, knowledge, his body unable to bear itself, his mind surrounded. The writer is considered immoral. The character in the tub of water is considered insane. History moves itself without art. Art clings like a parasite, or the neurological paths hidden in the spine.

day and night, night and day

A crack of light splits her cornea or skull as if with a knife. The dark explodes into light. A soft edged blur in…a doorway? Her eyes tear and tear. She closes them against light. Her arms reach out. A moan. He takes her into his arms, carries her out of the dark. Small wailings.

A room with the dimmest of light. The smell of sandalwood. Candles. She is lowered as gentle as a whisper into a tub of very warm water. Scent. Her hair is washed anonymously from behind. Her head rests on the edge of a porcelain tub. Her jaw is taut. Her lips slightly parted. Smell inside her, around her, womb.

She is left there for one half hour.

She is lifted from the tub and carried to a sofa. Rested there as if precious cargo. A fur across her body. She recognizes his smell, though she is still blind.

Fingers in her mouth. She sucks and spit fills the hole and fingers tasting of sweet and more sweet and around her mouth a little down her throat and again and again. The same fingers into her anus and back to the mouth and the ass and back and forth like that. Sweet as brandy or peach. Her nipples harden.

He removes the fur. Her body is amber glow. Forgetting itself.

Memoriless. Her wrists are bound with a satin tie, she can feel this precisely. Her legs are spread. Each ankle is taken tenderly between hands, bound with satin ties. Her sight returns to the head slowly, slowly. A man in a white wig; blue satin clothing. Hands as tender as birth.

174

Her cunt is wide, opening and opening, lips sucking apart, legs pulling their tendons toward life.

He enters her for hours; a long thick candle. The flame lit again and again. A wooden truncheon. A hand. Tongue. A silver rod. Fruit or vegetable or some solid large food. He eats, passes wet food to her mouth to mouth. The neck of a bottle of champagne. Foam and cold entering her. He drinks from her mouth.

She is left alone for one hour. She drifts to sleep.

People enter the room. She is untied, a man enters her quickly from behind, a woman sucks her nipples, bites, draws a bit of blood, laughing. He thrusts into her while the man is still taking her from behind. Women kiss and fondle her, lips, tits. Laughing.

She is so filled with joy her teeth unloose themselves inside of her mouth in an ocean of saliva, like the sea overtaking a ship or the mind, like the body turning back to its breathable blue deep, like oxygen melting into give.

history lessens

A woman says this: The most interesting modern theater is a theater which goes beyond psychology. Her pencil breaks at the white cusp of a page. It is nothing.

A man says this: We need true action, but without practical consequences. It is not on the social level that the action of theater unfolds. Still less on the ethical and psychological levels.... This obstinacy in making characters talk about feelings, passions, desires, and impulses of a strictly psychological order, in which a single word is to compensate for innumerable gestures, is the reason theater is dead. Figures must be freed from psychological and dialogue painting of the individual. He has been institutionalized already.

A man writes a play in which "realism" is transcended by "insanity." Modernism begins to borrow things from his private body without permission.

Language. Incantation. Exchange. Details of an execution. Dismemberment. An audience is listening. The world turns.

The phrase "the work of art" becomes political. Many people are frustrated and unhappy at having to think. 175

Neither moral nor aesthetic. Humanism's other face.

Speaking in fragments untethers. She knows this. So does he. All of them.

white

There is an ice pick and a huge chunk of dissolving ice—I say "dissolving" and not "melting" for the room is cold, the air cuts with each breath, cold as the white outside, the winter, the edges of inside and outside dissolving in cold and white breaking. Her arm raises as in a murder scene again and again and her face distorted by fatigue or cold or the mind dull numbing into blind. She has been in this room for two weeks, no food, no clothing, no heat. The furniture in the room is what we think of when we say "opulent." The tapestries, the velvet, the gold ornate carvings, paintings and silver, windows barred but huge, majestically open, beautiful. The carpet a bear's head, hand-painted tiles from India. Giant fireplace barren. She is screaming with her mouth but no sound comes out, the mouth and the throat having lost voice days and days ago.

She has sucked the block of ice again for sustenance.

She has mounted the block of ice in furious grotesque sexuality.

She has not killed herself; this interests the watchers. The ice pick was so obvious, and they even laid bets as to which day she would do it. Would she stab herself in the eye? This was an idea debated with much consternation. Surely the heart. Her longing frozen and dead, unable to bear her desire, to pierce the muscle.

But she had not done it, not then, not after starvation set in, not when she went from sobbing to hysterical laughing to rage, not when she sat in a drooling and freezing heap in the corner eating small bits of bear fur from the carpet, not when she shit the last of her body's waste into the fireplace, covering it with a tapestry over and over again, not when she knocked her head against the bars of the window dully for twenty hours in a row, until her head, bruised and beyond bleeding, closed itself to night.

When the door finally opens to human she is not of this world. She is play. No, pale, we meant to say pale.

writing

"I have laughed aloud in the writing of this. I understood long ago that I could not utter a phrase, or a single word, that was in any sense "descriptive" of the events which transpired so uselessly named in "my life." I saw immediately what the consequences would be and I saw as immediately how my attempting to contain my opportunity into discussion or description would kill any chance I would ever have. Don't you see? It would be as if one could travel into space and rediscover night and planet and self. I saw that. I retain a great sense of pride for having seen that. For realizing I might witness or give witness to the body in a way no woman ever had. That I might have access to a knowledge out of the world of my gender's experience. Friends, relatives, pregnant, husbands, children. At the point at which I thought I might vomit myself out, release myself to some river or pill or knife's edge, he came. Not as a lover or desirous of me as an object."

She wipes sweat from her upper lip and moves in her chair as slowly as molecules of air around a gesture.

"I was nearly struck dumb with the simplicity."

176

Her hand is cramping, or is it her eyes? She looks toward the door and back to the page and up and down like that too often. Her temples thud. Her hand aches.

"I want to write down in a sentence or two the first moments. Not to remember them. I haven't the slightest interest in nostalgia. Neither have I an interest in recording events for anyone or for myself. I want to write the sentences as a form of surrender, so that I need not worry about containing the chaos of my body, so that the grammar might hold what I cannot. I am no longer able to hold the sense. I want to let go. I want to go. I am choosing a wordless being. I do not want my I. I release it, I give it back to the world."

Her hand quivers violently. She calms it through will or love. No, not love. Never love. Her will. She begins.

"A night in November. A hand, a knife at the throat. A cut, night, cold, from jaw to shoulder blade. I do not cry out—this is the miracle. Nothing he ever does is as enormous as this thing I did to myself. This silence not from pain or from submission or from fear but from desire. Nor do I die from this wound. He stays with me for seven days, nursing me as if I am the tiniest bone of a child. I am beautiful beyond words. I am written, devoted."

The door brings him into vision. Her hand ceases. She closes the book, the pen is at rest. Her eyes the world.